How DIDN'T *She* KNOW?

What you won't do for love

(Book

D1600838

PATRICE PAGE

Follow me on Instagram

@tresse_n_credible

Like me on Facebook

@Author Patrice Page

Thank you so much for reading my book, "How Didn't She Know?" It means so much to me to know that my story has reached you, and I'm so grateful to be able to share my work with you.

Your reviews are critical to other readers and me. By writing a review, you are helping to spread the word about my book and empowering others to do the same!

Thank you again for reading my book and investing your time. I genuinely appreciate your support.

ACKNOWLEDGMENTS

I dedicate this book to my family and friends who encouraged me to continue writing because you saw my vision; I love you. Kimberly, my sister—you're my rock; Shavonne, my cousin, you should get paid for nagging.

To my readers, I hope this novel is entertaining enough where your loyalty will have you purchase the trilogies to see how the story ends.

Finally, I dedicate this book to Blu, the only color fitted to color the sky, especially to you.

TABLE OF CONTENTS

Chapter One

ESSENCE

It's now, or never, I thought to myself as I sat in my silver Tesla in the parking structure of the Detroit Riverside Casino Hotel, staring at the GPS app. It showed the coordinates of Christian Powell, my husband. I had been contemplating the possibility that he'd been having an affair. I tracked his movements all day, determined to get to the bottom of his disappearing acts, and had been sitting in my car for 30 minutes going over my marriage and the events leading me here.

Christian awakened at dawn, showered, and dressed before leaving our Farmington Hills home before the sun was up. He told me he would be out of town for business but lying had become a regularity. We were newlyweds. You would think we should still be in the honeymoon phase having the time of our lives, but Christian had been distant in the last few months.

When we first married, we would have sex regularly, he'd surprise me with flowers for no reason, and we had date night three times a week to keep the spark going. Our friends would even use our union as an example of relationship goals, but suddenly, all that stopped.

Christian was a successful attorney who worked at my father's law firm Dickerson-Bradly Law. I was a successful interior decorator; we were doing well financially. Our marriage was almost perfect until I got baby fever. I often daydreamed about starting a family with my husband. It would get so terrible that I would be in the middle of a conversation and think of babies. When I was alone in my room, I'd stand in front of the mirror, placing a throw pillow under my shirt, wondering how I would look pregnant. I even started searching the Internet for baby names. But ever since I mentioned wanting to start a family, we had sex less. We argued more when I noticed that we were not spending much time together and changes in his daily routine; he'd become evasive and highly offended by my assumption that he was cheating or uninterested in having a baby. Christian's go-to response, "I'm swamped with cases," was always his comeback, but what else was I to think?

My thoughts quickly shifted from babies to Christian cheating. He must have been having sex with somebody because he barely touched me. A website suggested using a GPS tracker to track your lover, so I ordered one, and it finally arrived. I read the directions and decided to stick it underneath his vehicle. Christian came home from work several hours later than usual again, which became the norm. I lay motionless in bed and pretended to snore before he walked into our main bathroom to shower. I waited until I heard the water run before I snuck out of bed and tip-toed downstairs to the garage. I got on my knees, stuck the GPS tracker to his car, hurried back upstairs, and got back underneath the covers, acting as if I was in bed the entire time sleeping, just in time for Christian to turn off the shower and get into bed. I stared at the wall listening to him snore while my beating heart raced and eventually put me to sleep.

The next morning, I ran my fingers through my untamed hair and pulled my sun visor down, looking at my bloodshot eyes. Exiting the Lodge freeway, I almost blew my cover after a car ran the stop sign. I managed to swerve just in time to avoid a collision. *Get it together,* I thought, hitting the steering wheel. I was ready to see what the hell Christian was up to, grabbing my black sunglasses from my purse and sliding them over my eyes. The wind was blowing hard from all of the rain, so I zipped up my black jogging suit jacket. My heart thumped against my chest. The closer I approached the elevator; I looked down at my GPS app. I headed to the second floor following his coordinates, which led me to room 233. I pretended to be a concierge standing outside the door. Putting my ear against the door, I couldn't hear anything. *Is he sleeping? Who the fuck is in there with him?* I thought. I banged on the door with my fist and started kicking it. I heard whispers, so I started knocking on the door again, harder this time, and Christian's voice rang out.

"Who is it?" he yelled from inside the room.

"It's me! Open this goddamn door," I shouted from the hall-way. "I thought you said you were out of town for business; YOU'RE A LIAR. Open the door. NOW!"

I heard tussling. The doorknob turned, and I pushed against the door, using all my weight to force my way into the room.

"Baby, I can explain," were the last words I heard him scream before my entire life changed. I stood in the middle of the dimly lit suite, not knowing if I should leave or kill my husband and this uncanny stranger standing next to him. I trembled and felt the hairs stand on the back of my neck. Christian lunged towards me, but I stepped back, and the door closed. I sprinted towards the elevator and heard the bell ring. I put my arm through the closing doors just in time, stepped inside, and pressed the button repeatedly, hoping the elevator would close before he arrived. Instead, I saw Christian through the small opening, with tears flowing from his eyes, "Essence, please don't go," he yelled before the elevator completely shut, closing him out of my life—for now.

"Essence, your acceptance letter came," I heard my mother Debra calling as I opened the door coming in from school. I attended Briarston High School in West Bloomfield, Michigan, one of the most prestigious high schools. Most people pegged me as an overachiever because I made all A's. I agreed, but I enjoyed having fun like the rest of my peers. My parents lectured me on the importance of getting good grades in hopes of receiving an academic and athletic scholarship. So, I stayed on top of my work, set goals, and read books during significant breaks and holidays. It put a lot of pressure on me, knowing that my parents were successful; my father was a retired football player-turned-attorney, and my mother was a successful interior decorator. So, I learned fast how to keep my priorities in check.

"Coming." Closing the door and throwing my bookbag to the floor, I ran toward the kitchen.

"Now, don't run in my house like this is one of those tracks. This letter is not going anywhere," my mother waved the acceptance letter, jokingly, in front of my face. "Where's my kiss?" she smiled, snatching the letter back out of my hand.

"Mom! Stop teasing – you know I've been waiting weeks for that," I pouted, kissing her on the cheek and hugging her from the side.

"Come on, baby, and we've been waiting on you to open the letter since it arrived," my father Franklin chimed in. "I want to know if my baby is a future Cadmus Cougar," sounding prideful, he placed his arm around my shoulder. He had attended Morrall College of East Lansing. During undergrad, he played football and earned the Heisman trophy. Growing up I heard so many stories about my father's undergraduate football career that it lit a fire in me. I became obsessed with track and field; I loved to run, and I was pretty damn fast. I ran 21.36 seconds in the 200-meter dash. The apple doesn't fall far from the tree because my father was book smart and athletic. He had what it took to go pro. Unfortunately, all his dreams ended during one of the biggest games of his junior year – the Morrall College versus the University of Meade of Ann Arbor game; two rival teams. It was only 2.17 seconds before Morrall College would be champions of the Rose Bowl. Unfortunately, my father collided with another player so hard that it left him with a neck injury, tarnishing his dreams. It took months to rehabilitate from the damage, and it was a miracle he could walk. My father was hurt learning he would never play football again, so he channeled all his anger and frustration into learning criminal law and earning his undergraduate law degree. After he graduated college, he studied for his LSAT, and Harrison Law accepted him into Law School. My father had made such a big name for himself during his football career that firms were willing to hire him in hopes his name and legacy would boost clients.

Smiling with excitement, I opened the letter. "Yes! I got a scholarship—they're offering me a full ride to Morrall College of East Lansing," I said, jumping up and down. I hugged both my parents and stared back at the letter.

"I knew it, baby," my mom opened the refrigerator, pulling out a specially made cake she ordered from the bakery. "Now it's time to celebrate."

"Mom, I'm going to pass on a slice right now. There's only a week until prom, and I'm watching my figure," I said, holding my stomach.

"Chile, a little piece of cake won't hurt you. Sit down and eat—I ordered your favorite," reaching for a knife and saucer to put a slice on. "See, it's not even that big," she smiled, placing the piece in front of me.

"That cake does look good, baby," my father added, "Cut me a slice, too, baby."

I scarfed the piece down so fast you would have thought I swallowed it whole. "I have homework," I said, getting up from the table.

I got into my room and plopped down on the bed, rummaging in my purse to grab my phone. My best friend, Madison, called. I kicked off my shoes and lay back on the bed, getting comfortable. "It's about time you called," she yelled into the phone, chewing gum in my ear. "You ready for the prom?"

I rolled my eyes. Madison knew damn well I hated when she chewed in my ear. "Before I answer the question, stop popping that gum in my ear. Yes, I'm ready for prom, are you?"

"You know I am, and I know you better be since you are going to prom with fine-ass Roderick. Good lawd, that boy is finer than a fried bologna sandwich. He might try to make a move on you, girl!"

"And I will quickly shut him down. He knows I'm a virgin, and just because he's fine doesn't mean he gets a ticket into these panties. Besides, if there's no ring on my finger, he not getting any of this," I held my hand in front of my face, looking at my finger. "And it's not."

"I don't know how you managed to be a virgin looking like you do," Madison's undertone made me feel a bit uncomfortable.

Slightly disgusted I responded, "Don't do me." We had been friends since elementary; like most adolescents, who experimented, Madison dabbled here and there with a few girls in high school. She knew I didn't get down like that, but despite her lifestyle, she and I remained close—as long as she didn't cross the line with me.

"Whatever," Madison said, sucking in air. "You know you're like one of the prettiest girls in school, is all I'm saying, so chill," she said with an attitude.

I was 5'6" with a slim, thick frame, and I loved what track did to my body. I inherited my hazel eyes from my father and my naturally curly hair from my mother. Most of the cute girls in high school were stuck up, but not me. I saw the beauty in everything and everyone, which attracted many people to my personality and helped me make many friends. My grandmother always told me that looks would only get you so far, but charm would get you out of trouble, even traffic tickets. I can't forget when she was pulled over on I-75 by a state trooper for speeding. She smiled and used her southern charm on that officer. So instead of giving my grandmother a ticket, he invited her to his church service.

"Guess what?" I blurted out. "I got my acceptance letter from Morrall," straying from the subject.

"Yes! Girl, I am so happy for you. I know they offered you a full ride, right?"

I yawned. "They did. Now you gotta hurry and get your letter so we can be roommates."

"Why do you say it all nonchalantly like you're unfazed? All I could remember when we were growing up is how much you wanted to be a Cadmus Cougar like your daddy."

"I'm happy, girl. But if we don't pass these finals, neither of us will attend Morrall College. Have you started studying? I heard the exam is 75% of the grade," I asked, concerned.

"I skimmed over the study guides, but it's so much information; I'm so nervous," Madison started pushing buttons in my ear.

"You know I can hear that, right?" I asked in an annoyed tone.

"Yeah, my bad, girl. Jhace is calling; let me call you back. We need to get to studying anyway." She was even more distracted.

"Alright, girl, talk to you later," I hung up the phone and grabbed my book bag. After four hours of studying, I called it a night.

Finals came and went, prom was three days away, and my dress still wasn't ready. Sitting in the family room, I saw my mother on the phone. I thought *she must be talking to Lorraine, Jackie, and Maxine, her best friends,* overhearing her discuss prom and my acceptance into Morrall College. She was so excited you'd think it was her prom.

A few months ago, she shared a story with me about how my grandparents couldn't afford to buy her a prom dress, and they forced her to wear her Easter dress, but she still won prom queen. Of course, prom wasn't a big deal for me, but I knew it meant a lot to her, so I pretended to be excited—especially when she turned the speakerphone on, putting me on the spot with her friends.

She finished her call, sat beside me, and ran her fingers through my curls. "Are you excited about prom, baby?"

I smiled, "More like nervous. But, Momma, why did you invite so many people over? You know how I get around big crowds and attention being on me."

"You'll be fine baby. I remember when I was younger—I didn't have anyone to see me off. So, you should be happy all these people want to come to spend this time with you."

"I know, but you always overdo it. I'm happy with it just being you, dad, and grandma."

"What about Maxine, Lorraine, and Jackie?" my mom looked taken aback.

Handing her the remote, "If that makes you happy, mom," I headed into the kitchen, hoping to avoid one of those long lectures she gives about family. I get it—family is everything.

My parents didn't have siblings. Before they conceived, she was pregnant with a son but lost the baby. It took my father years of convincing her to try again, and after years of counseling, she agreed. Ecstatic, she delivered a healthy baby, much more a girl; my mother overdid many things. Sometimes, I felt smuggled by her. Don't get me wrong, I love and appreciate her, but it's frustrating when she tries to live life vicariously through me.

Barely moving her eyes from the evening news, she turned the television up louder. It was a breaking news story about Detroit's hottest rap artist, DEFiant, getting a weapons and drug possession charge. The media was swarming everywhere, trying to get a statement from his attorney, my dad, who happened to be representing him.

"Momma, turn that up a little bit." Walking back into the family room, I sat next to her on the couch. I couldn't believe daddy was representing DEFiant; I was utterly amazed.

"Who is that baby?" My mother squinted her eyes, "Deliverance? I know that's not his name," she said, chuckling.

"No Ma, that's DEFiant, you know that song *One Track Mind*, that's him," I recited some of the lyrics.

"Deliverance is a better name for him right now. It's gone take God and your father to get him out of that mess," she said, pointing at the television. "Look at your daddy! Isn't he handsome?"

My brows furrowed, "Does this mean that daddy won't be here to see me off for prom?" As might be expected, I'm a daddy's girl; his being at my prom send-off was significant even though I could care less about prom.

"Yes, your daddy said that he would be here. He's excited to see you off, Honey. Don't worry, your pretty little head."

My cell phone vibrated; it was Roderick calling. "Hey, what's up?" I smiled, turning my attention from the news. He and I had been dating for two years, and anytime I spoke with him, I got butterflies; he was so smooth.

"Hey beautiful, do you want to go to Jhace's house after the prom? He's throwing an afterparty since his parents won't be there?"

"I need permission to go, but I don't think they will go for that, especially since his folks won't be there."

Chuckling, "Leave it to me. Your dad likes me, and I'll tell him you'll be home at a decent hour."

"Madison and I talk daily, she hasn't mentioned this, especially if she expects to see me there."

"It's last minute, so that's why she hasn't told you yet. Plus, it's invitation-only Jhace didn't want the party to get out of control."

"Before I forget, my mom is going all out over prom, so don't be surprised by all the photographers."

Roderick laughed. "More like paparazzi. I'm cool—I'm looking forward to making it a night to remember," he said, ending the call.

That boy, I tell you. He could talk his way out of a paper bag if he wanted to. I'd be lying if I said I hadn't thought about sleeping with him on prom night. I'd been holding onto my virginity by the skin of my teeth. He was FOINE! He was 6'3", milk chocolate, muscular, jet-black, low haircut, thick eyebrows, long eyelashes that all the girls loved, including me, and pearly white teeth. He was a smooth talker too, and it didn't help that he was the star quarterback for our football team.

Before making it official, all the girls talked about wanting to sleep with him, but he never gave them attention. I was shocked when he finally asked me out. He seemed focused on his football career just as I was on track, which attracted me to him. Plus, he never pressured me to have sex, and two months passed before we had our first kiss. I believe in the man taking the lead, but I planned on taking charge if we'd gone out for one more date without me getting a kiss. I began to think he wasn't interested. When I told Madison about it, she was just as relieved as I was. You'd think he kissed her too! I laughed thinking about it. I was lucky enough to have the privilege of being with a gentleman.

The next three days flew by, and mom ran around the house, ensuring every detail was in order. She hired a celebrity makeup artist; I was impressed. I stared into the mirror, barely noticing my reflection. *Beautiful*, I thought. I felt like I was seeing myself for the very first time.

"Essence, guests are arriving," my mother called upstairs.

Harlem shouted, "I am almost done, Debra," she finished her last-minute touches to my hair, "You look stunning, girl! Fit for a queen." She stepped away, marveling at her masterpiece.

My mother gasped, "Oh my God," holding her hand over her mouth as she watched me walk downstairs, "Baby, you are…" signaling the photographer, not completing her statement, "Take a mother-daughter shot, please." Her eyes watered, "You're gorgeous."

I smiled, "Thank you, mom." Everyone followed suit and began showering me with compliments and waiting for their turns to take a picture with me.

"I think I see Roderick pulling up," she said, looking out the door.

"Knock, knock," Roderick announced before entering the house. The look on his face was priceless when he laid eyes on me. His mouth dropped wide open, and a fly could have flown into it. Roderick broke his trance when my mother told him to take a few pictures.

Whispering, "You look exquisite," he stood behind me with his arms wrapped around my waist. His penis pressed against my ass, and instantly my heart pounded faster.

"What's wrong, baby? You look flushed," my mother walked towards me, fanning a magazine in front of my face.

"Nothing, mom. I see dad pulling up." I was happy my father made it home with just enough time to see me off. He always showed me what a gentleman looked like entering the house with all-white roses and a box of my favorite candy. I rushed towards him and kissed him on the cheek, not worried if I was smearing my lipstick.

"Hey, sorry I'm late," he hugged me. Then, he turned to Roderick, giving him a handshake, "Isn't my princess beautiful?" he asked Roderick.

Grinning from ear to ear, Roderick replied, "Yes, she is, Mr. Donaldson."

"What time are you planning on having her back home?" he quizzed, "I don't want to hear about you having her inside some hotel room."

"No, sir! I respect Essence," Roderick turned, looking me in the eyes before facing my dad. "1:00 AM, I was hoping that you wouldn't mind if we could go to an afterparty; Jhace's mother is throwing a party for the graduating varsity seniors." Reaching into his pocket, Roderick pulled out a piece of paper, "Here's my cell phone number and Jhace's mom's."

My dad turned to me, giving me a trusting look many parents give their children when they hope that all their life lessons have sunk in, "That'll be fine if there's no drinking, and I will confirm with Jhace's mom."

Smiling, Roderick said, "Let's get going," looking at the clock, I noticed we were running late. As I stepped into the limousine I thought, *I hoped the student body hadn't announced the king and queen.*

We'd made it just in time to take pictures, and the DJ started playing *Happily Ever After* by Case; *this is my song*, I thought. Roderick took my hand and led me to the dance floor. It seemed he read my mind because I was dying to dance. Roderick started singing in my ear, and I loved his singing. My head lay against his chest as we swayed to the music; he smelled good. I was in a spell, dancing in his arms. His cologne excited me, and I wondered how it felt to be intimate with him. Then, my mind drifted to seeing him naked, and my clitoris throbbed feeling Roderick's penis harden. He leaned down, pressing his lips against mine softly, slightly parting my lips to caress his tongue against mine.

We were still dancing slowly when the song stopped, and the crowd started circling us. The ballroom echoed when everyone at prom said, "Awe," knocking us out of our trance.

Mr. Geter stepped on stage, tapping the microphone, and clearing his throat. "This year's prom king and queen will be," he opened the envelope and read the names but waited a few minutes to build the suspense, "Roderick and Essence." We both kissed, and Roderick grabbed my hand, escorting me to the stage for Mr. Geter to crown us King and Queen.

Madison ran over to me, jumping in excitement. "I'm so happy; I knew y'all would win. Y'all are such a cute couple."

"Thank you, Madison," I reached out to hug her, "What time is the party going to start at Jhace's?"

"We were waiting on the king and queen announcement before leaving." Madison looked at her phone, "We should go 'cause it's almost 10:30 PM." Jhace and Roderick walked over at the perfect time, "We were just saying we were ready to go," Madison wrapped her arm around Jhace's arm.

"Let's bust a move then," Roderick took my hand and led us all to the limousine. Minutes later, we pulled up to the house, cars stretched around the block, "Dang man, how many people are here?" he looked out of the window.

"The word spread fast when they heard I had the keys to the palace," Jhace said in astonishment.

"Wait a minute," I looked at Roderick. "You said a small party? What if my dad calls?"

"Don't worry, baby," Roderick dapped Jhace's hand, "I gave your dad his sister's phone number—she's hella cool."

"Yeah, don't worry," Jhace cosigned as he got out of the limo, then helping Madison out.

The house was smoky, and drinks were everywhere. Then, finally, Roderick and Jhace walked away, and Madison and I stood in the center of the room wide-eyed, "Did you expect it to be *this* many people?"

"Calm down, Essence," Madison rubbed my back, "Jhace did invite a lot of people, but you're good. Let's go take those seats over there," she pointed at the sofa.

Roderick and Jhace reappeared with some red plastic cups and said in unison, "Here you ladies go."

Looking into my cup, I asked, "What is this?" I eyed the liquid concoction, and I wondered what was in the drinks, "My dad told me never to drink anything someone hands me if I don't see them open it."

Roderick took the cup and drank a sip, "Do you seriously think I'm going to give you something laced with drugs? You know me better than that," he said, handing me back the cup.

Madison took a sip, "Damn, Jhace, this is good—you made it?"

"My sister made it; she has two barrels of this shit," he said, chuckling over his sister's willingness to supply alcohol.

"Taste it, Essence, it's prom. Don't be so stuck up," Madison turned up her nose.

I took another look in the cup. Apprehensive, I took a drink, not wanting to spoil the night. Cracking a smile, I said in amazement, "This is good." I took another gulp, emptying the entire cup.

"Slow down, baby! It's mixed with Everclear," Roderick sounded worried by how fast I swallowed the liquor. Then he laughed. "I know it tastes fruity, but it's some alcohol in there. I don't want you getting too drunk."

Biting my lip, I asked flirtatiously, "Should I be worried about you taking advantage of me?"

Roderick grinned, taking my cup away; he went into the kitchen to grab another drink, "Y'all think you could behave if Jhace and I go hang out with the team for a few?" He gave us puppy dog eyes, and he knew I had difficulty saying no to that.

Tilting her head to the side, Madison demanded, "Don't have us sitting here all night!" She then gave Jhace the side eye.

Madison and I sat there laughing about all the crazy shit we observed; we drank two more cups of jungle juice. Then, looking at my phone, I saw it was close to 12:00 AM. I panicked, "What's wrong?" Madison slurred, buzzing off the drinks.

"Girl, it's almost time for me to go. Roderick has been gone for a while, and I can't afford to miss curfew," I grabbed my purse to search for him.

"Damn, Essence, why you gotta go from zero to one hundred that fast? It's not 12:30 AM yet," Madison followed behind me but stumbled backward, falling back into her seat.

"Girl, sit your drunk ass down—I'll find him myself," I walked to the patio door and opened it. I saw every varsity player, except him, outside by the hookah.

"Have y'all seen Roderick?" I yelled at Jhace and the other players.

Jhace exhaled a puff of smoke, "Naw, last he mentioned, he said he was going back in the house to check up on you."

I walked back into the house, scanning the living room; I saw Madison passed out on the couch. Peeping my head into the kitchen, I didn't see him in the crowd. *Where is this boy?* I thought, heading upstairs, "Roderick," I walked in on a couple having sex in one of the bedrooms. I immediately closed the door. *Damn, I have to use it,* I thought, shifting left and right, trying to hold my urine. Then, without knocking, I turned the bathroom knob, "FUCK!" I rubbed my eyes; I'd been drinking and was hoping I was tripping, "What the fuck!" I hollered, watching Roderick thrust his hips back and forth, gripping another guy's shoulders as he dug deep into his ass.

He stepped back, revealing his erection; his penis pointed straight out. I turned around and took off running as Roderick reached down, trying to pull his pants up. He started to chase me.

"Baby, wait, wait, wait," he repeated, trying to stop me.

I was in pure disgust. I didn't want to hear shit. I walked in on Roderick fucking Brandon, a varsity senior who allegedly was on the down low.

"I don't want to hear shit you got to say, Roderick. You are giving backshots to him and lying to me! You had me bragging about you being a gentleman who respected my boundaries and me, but all this time you been fucking him," I said, pointing my finger. I ran downstairs, "Wake up, Madison," I grabbed her arm.

Madison rubbed her eyes. "What's wrong?" She immediately looked at me and then to Roderick, who stood at the bottom of the stairs fixing his pants. "It wasn't good?" She assumed I was disappointed about having sex with Roderick.

I pointed at Roderick and Brandon, who followed him downstairs with a sinister look. "Ask them," I shouted.

"Ask me what?" Brandon shouted back. "I'm sure you don't want to know how good it feels for your boyfriend to be fucking ME in the bathroom while his pretty little princess was one flight beneath us. I'm surprised it took you that long to find Roderick with all that moaning and groaning he was doing. That boy blew my back out," he laughed.

"Shut the fuck up, B. Why the fuck is you lying?" Roderick looked at me, and then at the crowd, "It's not what you think, Essence—I can explain," he walked closer to me.

Everyone had their eyes glued on us like a soap opera, watching what was unfolding. Even the couple I walked in on having sex was heading downstairs to get a closer view. *So, I guess that nut wasn't as good as what was going down*, I thought.

"Am I dreaming," Madison said, pinching herself on the arm. "What the hell is going on, Essence? I know I had a few drinks and dozed off, but what the hell did I wake up to?"

"What you woke up to is me finding Roderick in the bathroom with this fuckboy, Brandon." Then directing the attention back at them, I continued, "Bent over the bathroom sink getting fucked by Roderick is what you woke up to." I grabbed her arm, "Let's go," we rushed through the crowded living room listening to the laughter and "hell no's" that filled the room.

I didn't bother looking back; I was embarrassed. How the hell didn't I know? *Finally*, I thought, opening the limousine door. "Take me home," I yelled at the driver. I rode the entire way in silence, too ashamed to look Madison in the eyes. By the time we arrived at my house, I was past curfew.

"Essence, are you okay?" Madison squeezed my hand. "Ready to go inside?"

"I'm good. I'm just…," Tears poured down my face. Madison wiped the tears from my cheeks. "I just don't understand."

"What is there to understand? You did nothing wrong, and there's no reason to be embarrassed. That's Roderick's problem. You do have a right to be angry; I would be. But girl, this isn't the end of the world." Madison stroked my hair, "I'm going to stay the night here. We can talk, or I can listen, but I don't want to leave you like this."

"Thanks, girl," I wiped the tears from my eyes. "Let me get myself together before I go inside. I can't believe I'm late. My dad is going to be PISSED." To my surprise, all the lights were off inside. "Come on," I whispered to Madison as I crept up to my room, "They're asleep."

With a smile on Madison's face, she whispered, "See, God's already working in your favor." She took off her shoes and snuck behind me.

We stayed up until the crack of dawn talking. I did most of the talking, and Madison did most of the listening between dozing off. "I think this is a sign, Madison. I'm going to save my virginity until I'm married," I said, laying my head on the pillow.

"Marriage...I hear you," Madison mumbled with her eyes closed, "You aren't tired yet?"

I turned the light off and slid beneath the covers. "Good night. Thanks for listening," I said before dozing off to sleep.

I opened my eyes and turned over; my room was empty. "Madison," I yelled, but I got no response. Grabbing my robe, I walked to the bathroom to brush my teeth and headed down to the kitchen. "It's about time you woke up," my mother said, reaching for a plate. "Madison was down here keeping me company while I cooked us breakfast."

Cutting my eyes at Madison, "How long have you been awake and talking to my mom," I asked nervously. You could never know what to expect from her, and it would be a nightmare if she told my mother what happened.

"Just 15 minutes. I woke up when I smelled that coffee brewing," Madison walked over to the coffee pot and poured herself another cup.

"I've been dying to hear about prom," my mom said, fixing herself a bagel. "Your father and I fell asleep early last night; I was trying to wait up and hear all about it."

Madison and I looked at each other before she blurted out, "Essence won prom queen! We enjoyed ourselves; the DJ had the music lit," she gave the clean short version of the evening.

"That is wonderful! I knew my baby would win." My mom ran her fingers through my curls. "Where's the crown? I want to see it!" She said with a huge smile on her face.

"Upstairs, mom, I'll grab it in a second." I was glad my mother could be an airhead at times, unable to read the room. She was so much into the glitz and glam she wouldn't dare think *I* had a horrible time. Running upstairs, I grabbed my crown and glanced in the mirror, pausing before heading back downstairs. I was so happy and on a natural high being named prom queen. *This crown means nothing to me,* I thought, never imagining my evening would come plummeting down.

She panted, looking at the crown, "This is so beautiful, baby—let me see it!" She grabbed it, placed it on her head, and stood in front of the mirror on the mantel. "She's your queen-to-be. A queen to be forever," she said, quoting the line from "Coming to America."

Madison and I burst into laughter, "Oh my gosh, mom. What in the world?" I grabbed my stomach from laughing so hard.

Taking off the crown, my mother handed it to me. "What? I am a queen." She walked back into the kitchen, taking a bite of her bagel, "Don't act like you don't know," she snapped her fingers.

"Mrs. Debra, you're so funny," Madison chimed in. "I love that movie; it's one of my favorites," Madison looked at me, "Can you take me home after breakfast?"

"Yeah. I can swoop you on my way to the gym. I need to run off some steam," I took a bite out of the toast and gulped down the orange juice.

After dropping Madison off, I headed to Get Your Fit On gym. My phone had been off, but I powered it on to listen to music while I ran. I rolled my eyes; 25 missed calls and 133 messages. *I don't have time for this,* I thought. I deleted the messages without reading any, plugged in my headphones, and started jogging on the treadmill. Thinking of Roderick having sex with Brandon made me instantly upset, and I sprinted until I noticed the mileage said I'd run eight miles within an hour. I cooled down and jogged for a few. Impressed by my workout, *I can't think of a time when I just ran like that,* I thought.

Just before I started doing some deadlifts, Roderick walked through the doors, "Essence, will you talk to me?" He walked towards me, his shirt was wrinkled, and his eyes were red.

"I don't have nothing to say to you, Roderick. You ruined my prom and lied to me! Besides, this isn't the damn place or the time," I dropped the free weights and grabbed a towel and bottle of water from my gym bag.

"When will it be a good time to talk? We have to talk about this Essence, please? I'm begging you," he reached out to grab my hand.

I quickly snatched my arm away, "No, we don't have anything to discuss. I'm over this, and frankly, I don't ever want to hear from you AGAIN; go be with your boyfriend." I grabbed my gym bag and headed towards the exit.

"Shhhhh," he placed his finger over his mouth, "Can we at least talk outside? I promise I won't take long," he pleaded.

I stopped and turned around, "You have five minutes—let's go." I walked to my car and placed my bag into the trunk, "What do you have to say?"

"Essence, I care about you so much, and I'm sorry that you had to see that. I don't know why I did it," tears flowed from Roderick's eyes.

I interrupted, "You don't know why you did it? That doesn't make sense to me. You're the only one that knows why you do what you do. You have to come up with something better or get out of my way, wasting more time. Three minutes," I shouted as I opened my car door.

"Essence, you don't gotta be so fucking mean, alright? It's hard for a BLACK man to acknowledge or admit he has thoughts about other men. I'm sure you understand," he looked me in the eyes, "I should have told you, but I tried to bury the thoughts thinking maybe it'll go away. I spoke to my church pastor and prayed several times about my sexuality. I liked you, and I thought that by dating you, I wouldn't feel this way anymore, but I guess...," he sobbed, "The last thing I wanted to do was to hurt you, and I was thinking of so many ways to tell you I may be bisexual, but I was afraid that you wouldn't want to be with me anymore."

"I hear you, Roderick, but I need to process this shit. Maybe I can learn to forgive you in the future, but I don't have anything to say to you right now. You hurt me, and my embarrassment last night has put me in a bad space. You could have just said you're questioning your sexuality; maybe I could have been a friend to you, but right now, I can't respect you for lying," I slammed the door and rolled the window down.

"I understand, and I hope you can forgive me in time. I am terribly sorry," Roderick said, wiping his face and walking away from my Monte Carlo.

"Yup," I said before pulling out of the parking lot.

The conversation with Roderick was more draining than the three hours I spent in the gym. The word about prom was spreading faster than wildfires. Students posted videos on social media of last night's drama. *I can't deal with this*, I thought, as I eyed my phone and saw the text messages from my classmates. Exhaling slowly, I headed to the bathroom to shower; *a new start is what I need*, I thought, thinking changing numbers would suffice, as I turned on the water and waited until the steam filled the bathroom.

Wrapping a towel around my body, I stood in the mirror and dried my hair, "Ugh, these people need to quit texting me," I scoffed, heading to my mother's bedroom.

"Mom, I need a new number," I stood at the foot of her bed and erased the last text threads.

She turned over and sat up in the bed, "What time is it?" she asked, looking at the clock hanging up on the wall, "New number? Why do you want to change it?"

I crossed my arms, "The last couple of days, someone's been calling my phone asking for someone named Robert," I wrinkled my brows, lying.

"Robert? Why would somebody be doing that?" She got out of bed, went into the bathroom, and shut the door behind her, "I don't care; I'll have it changed."

"Thanks, mom," I yelled through the door and went back to the bathroom to apply some hair products to keep my curls popping.

Doing my hair could be an all-day affair; *whew*, I thought, flopping down on my bed, I called Madison to give her my new number, but after one ring, Madison sent me to voicemail, "Call me girl," I rolled my eyes, and I hung up. Minutes later, she called; I answered, "Girl, are you screening calls?"

"I was wondering who this was calling from this unknown number," sounding confused, "Whose phone are you using to call me?"

"Mine, girl, I been getting calls and texts all day. I'm so over it," I sneered, "My mom changed it for me." I laid on my bed to get comfy, "Why did Roderick come to the gym looking for me, crying, trying to explain himself?" I nodded, "Madison, I have never been so depleted; this is my senior year—I'm supposed to be having fun, graduating. Now, I'm stressed worrying about this mess! I'm glad we didn't have sex," my voice started cracking.

"Mm-hmm, me too. Roderick needs to leave you alone and worry about his reputation. He's lied to many people; Jhace said that everyone was talking about that shit when we left his party," she sounded annoyed.

"Everybody probably thinks I'm stupid," I sobbed.

"Forget what everybody thinks," she inhaled and released an exasperated sigh, "I was just as shocked as you."

Sounding defeated, "I wish I could just go to sleep and wake up at college already," I wiped my tears and changed the subject, "What are you doing?"

"Nothing, girl. Jhace and I just returned from the movies. He's been getting on my nerves talking about his boy Roderick," she sucked her teeth, "I'm 'bout tired of hearing about it, no offense. But don't get me wrong, I know how it can be when you're questioning your sexuality; it is scary. You remember how I was when I told you that I liked girls?"

"Mm-hmm, I remember," I said, trying to follow her point.

"I was scared as FUCK," she chuckled, "I just don't like that he lied to you and didn't give you a chance to decide if you wanted to continue being with him."

Madison had more insight into LGBTQ issues and had her fair share of stigmas associated with her, and being her friend helped me to be more sensitive and understanding along the way. Still, I don't have that much forgiveness regarding dishonesty and lying as fuckboys; gay or straight. "Let's stop talking about this. I'm getting all worked up again," I felt the knots start to form in my stomach.

"I'm just ready to graduate and start training for the fall," I said, looking over my acceptance letter. "Girl, they got me staying in the athletic dorm," I rolled my eyes, imagining living with a stranger.

"You ready for early move-in," Madison asked, seeming to have perked up.

"Yup, one month, and I'm out of here!" We chuckled, "Alright, girl, I got to go," I hung up, and a rush of excitement came over me from thinking that I'll soon be away and doing what I love. *But first, I have to get through graduation and summer, and then I'm off!* The thought made the biggest smile come upon my face.

The following month flew by, and it was the morning of move-in day. My dad had been packing the U-Haul hatch to drive up to Morrall College of East Lansing since dawn.

"I can't believe it's time! I'm nervous," I bit my nails; ugh, a nasty habit I never broke.

"Why? You should be excited, get up there and do a good job; stay focused on school and track," he said, wrapping his arm around my shoulder, "When you get homesick, I'll pick you up," my father took the last of my boxes and shut the trunk of his Expedition.

Sucking in my teeth, "I can't believe I have to wait a year to have a car on campus; this sucks!" I pouted, hopping into the truck.

"Everything you need is on that campus—you can wait a year, chile," my mom said, handing me a jacket, "We should get on the road so we can get up there and get you unpacked. I booked a room so your father and I can stay overnight."

The ride felt like the longest ride of my life; I was excited to get to campus. The closer we got; I was wide-eyed as I saw Harrison Road billboards. "The campus is huge," I was in awe driving down to the dormitory, pointing out the window. "There's my dorm," I said with a smile.

"I know where it is—I'm an alumnus," he laughed and parked on the sidewalk to start unpacking.

Looking at the students coming in and out of the building, *those must be athletes*, I thought. "School doesn't start until August, right?" my mother asked, looking at all the students on campus.

"Yeah, but all the athletes live here," I said, walking into the hall to check in and get my key. The building smelled like freshly waxed floors, and the floors gleamed. I inhaled and exhaled slowly; I felt destined to be here. Grabbing the key, I noticed the most handsome guy from the corner of my eye, walking through the hall. We made eye contact before I exited the building. My heart palpated. I had never seen anyone as exotic looking as him; chiseled arms, wavy hair, colored eyes. He smiled, revealing the deepest dimple, and looked as though he was 6'5". Turning back, I stumbled as I missed a step.

My mother saw me as I slipped. "Are you okay, baby?" She sat at the back of the Expedition, fanning herself and drinking water.

"Yeah, I tripped. I saw some bins the boxes can go into to move me in faster; let me grab them." I ran towards the building, hoping I'd catch another glimpse of the mystery guy.

"No, baby, I will go grab it. Besides, I have to use the bathroom. Help your dad unload the U-Haul," she said as she walked into the dorm and returned 20 minutes later with a bin and two student-athletes willing to assist.

"Sorry I took so long. I was inside telling these nice gentlemen I was helping my daughter, who's also an athlete, move into the dorm, and they decided to help us load the bins," she smiled at me.

Shaking my head, "Thanks, mom." I looked down before rolling my eyes.

"Where are your manners, Essence—aren't you going to introduce yourself?" Pointing, "This is Bruce and, I'm sorry young man, what did you say your name is again?" she asked the other guy.

"Erik, ma'am," he said and looked at me.

"I'm Essence, and this is my father." I pointed to my dad, who walked up, wiping his hands on his jeans before extending his hand.

"I'm Franklin," he shook their hands.

Bruce almost knocked down Erik stepping closer, with excitement, "Thee Franklin Donaldson?"

"Yes, that's me," my father gripped Bruce's hand tighter, smiling wider. My dad loved the attention. He intentionally wore a Cadmus Cougar jersey with his number on the back to be more recognizable.

"Wow, sir, I can't believe it! Is it okay if I take a picture with you?" Bruce pulled out his cell phone. "I have to tell all my friends; they won't believe this."

After taking a few pics, I scoffed, "Dad, can we please start moving the stuff upstairs? The sooner we do it, the sooner we will be done." I interrupted the photoshoot, frustrated.

The evening was approaching, and we managed to get everything unpacked. I was hot and sweaty and desperately wanted to shower and explore the campus. Sounding anxious, "So, what time are you guys checking into the hotel?"

My dad laughed, "You trying to get rid of us already? I can imagine what it's going to be like when you start meeting new people and getting acclimated with the campus. We probably barely hear from you," he patted me on the back.

Tilting my head to the side, smiling, "Daddy, you know that's not true."

Chiming in, my mom said, "When I went to college, I came home every weekend," she gave me the side eye.

I placed my hand over my mouth and yarned, "I get the point," revolted by how sticky I felt, "I need to change clothes. What time are you checking out of the hotel tomorrow?"

"Eleven AM," my father said, looking at his watch. "Come on, Debra, let's go so this child of ours can change." He kissed my forehead and hugged me goodbye.

My mother followed suit. *Thank God,* I thought. I locked the door and grabbed my phone to call Madison. "Girl, I cannot wait until you get to Morrall. The campus is huge! Guess what, though?" I pursed my lips.

"Girl, what? Tell me." She didn't even bother guessing.

"I saw this fine-ass guy today. He was so damn handsome I almost fell down the stairs, not paying attention. Talk about awkward." I burst out in laughter. "Hello?" I looked at the phone to ensure my cell didn't drop the call, "Madison?"

"Girl, yeah, I'm here. I couldn't breathe laughing at your crazy ass. I could only imagine your dorky ass; I hope he didn't see you." She giggled, "How can you be quick on your feet running track but clumsy off the track? After Roderick, I thought you would focus on school and running?"

"I am, but I got eyes and can *still* look, Madison," shaking my head, sulking, "But he is *so* fine," I proceeded to describe him.

"Damn, let me hurry up and get there. If a third of guys looked like that, I don't know if I'd be able to continue dating Jhace," Madison sounded doubtful.

"If you love him, these dudes won't even matter. Besides, you have a good thing going, so don't mess it up all over a handsome face," I assured her.

"So true. I check into my room assignment in August, so you have two months to learn all the hot spots on campus for us to hang out. I was thinking about visiting you Friday to see how your dorm looks," Madison changed subjects.

"That'll be cool. I can't wait to see you, girl. We can go off campus to see where the malls are too." *I can't go without retail therapy for long*, I thought.

"Will do. I'm 'bout to head out and grab some food with Jhace. Catch up with you in a few," she hung up.

I placed my phone on the charger and took my clothes off to shower. I thought, *the water felt so damn good*, stepping under the showerhead. Water poured down my body, and I was in a daze, rubbing my breasts and nipples, thinking of the good-looking guy. Although I'm a virgin, I have been finding my way around my body for a few years. My hands wandered until my fingers found my clitoris. I rubbed it in circles, I trembled, and my knees buckled. Moans filled the empty bathroom; I was climaxing. I placed my hand over my mouth, trying to be quiet. Is this what it's going to be like all semester? Me masturbating, thinking of a stranger? I thought, picking up my shower gel to clean myself up.

Chapter Two

CHRISTIAN

Fanning myself from the heat, "Ava, why does it take you forever to get ready?" I sat on her bed, "I told you I'd be here an hour ago and purposely waited an extra 30 minutes before arriving."

She stuck her head out of the bathroom, "And you can keep waiting. You ain't got nothing to do," she snickered.

I walked over to her dresser, looking at the photos of Ava and me. Then, shaking my head, I thought, *another lifetime ago. I looked so different*, glancing at the high school graduation picture I had signed and given her, thinking I was the next Allen Iverson. My hair was long, corn rolled, I wore braces, and my facial hair hadn't grown yet.

Ava and I met in the fifth grade. We both played on basketball leagues, but different teams. She was such a girlie girl, and watching her play basketball was funny. She knew how to handle the ball but needed help with her crossover. So one day, I showed her the proper technique; since then, we have been thick as thieves.

In high school, everyone thought we had a thing for each other, often catching hell from her boyfriend, who disagreed we were only friends. I can't lie—she was attractive, but I never wanted to ruin our friendship by crossing the lines. Besides, I was already dealing with my growing pains and didn't have time to deal with any extra drama. The closer we got, it felt right to be friends, which was a good choice; it was easy to talk to Ava, and she understood me the most.

"I heard Coach Johnson was trying to scout you! Did you put thought into playing for Coach?" Ava walked out of the bathroom and sat down next to me.

"I thought about it, but I doubt I'll play. I ain't feeling basketball anymore," I rubbed my growling stomach, "Plus, I'm not in the best shape anymore."

"Boy, if you don't shut your ass up — you're still in shape. But, of course, it would help if you played all that talent going to waste," Ava said, grabbing her purse.

"Ava, I'm not playing," I cut her off mid-sentence, hoping she got the point, "I'm not gonna to play again. I want to focus on school, and that's it. My GPA fell, and I need to get accepted

944 094

into the law program. Last I checked, being a great basketball player wasn't a prerequisite," I laughed, walking to the door, "Now where we 'bout to eat at?"

We chuckled, "I got a taste for Pasadena Chicken. Let's go eat there." Ava put her lipstick on, grabbed her purse, and pushed past me to lock the door.

"I'm cool with that. We can eat anywhere at this point," my stomach rumbled.

"Is that you, sounding like that over there?" Ava looked at me, her brows creased, "Did you eat anything today?"

"Yeah, right before I went to the gym. But I burned off all that food. Hold up a second," I grabbed my phone from my pocket, reading the caller ID, "This moms," I answered the call and got into my blue Jeep. "Hey, Mom, what you doing?"

My mother was one of my biggest cheerleaders; she supported me in sports, school, and any decisions I made. Yet, at five years old, my mom explained that I was adopted; I hadn't known what the word biological meant at the time, but even though she wasn't my real mother, I loved her like she was. A few years later, I wanted to find my birth parents, and without hesitation, she looked over the paperwork and contacted the adoption agency to see if they had records, but we failed to find them. So finally, after several years of searching, I gave up and took it as a blessing that Geraldine Powell adopted me; she was a biological mother as far as I was concerned.

"Alrighty, Mom, I got to go—Ava and I are pulling up to Pasadena Chicken to eat. I love you, Mom!" I said, hanging up the phone.

"Pasadena!" Ava sang, bouncing her shoulders up and down and walking into the restaurant. "I hope they got fresh chicken wings out. I'm 'bout to kill some wings and salad," she said, grabbing a plate and proceeding to the buffet area.

Halfway into eating, I remembered I wanted to tell Ava about girlie from earlier, "I saw this BAD chic moving into your dorm today," I grinned, dipping my wings into ranch dressing.

"For real?" She sounded excited, taking a bite into her chicken wing, "Does this mean your ass is gonna be in my hall stalking this chic?" she asked playfully.

Chocking on my food, I took a sip of pop, "Stalking? Hell no! I ain't pressed," I said confidently, shoving her on the shoulder, "You play too much!" I chuckled, "She was fine, though. How 'bout, she damn near fell on her ass walking out the building from staring at me. I had to hold my laugh in until I got on the elevator," I crouched over and held my stomach laughing.

Ava winced, holding her hand over her mouth, "Oh man, damn, that's embarrassing. I'm glad you didn't laugh." She took a sip of sweet tea, "I wonder what sport she plays?"

"Resident Aide, you can find out," I smiled, knowing she was the plug.

"Humph, don't use me," she pursed her lips. "So, you trying to holla at her?" she questioned, sounding intrigued.

I gulped down some more pop, "Maybe," I smirked, "Ava, c'mon now, find out who she is and give your boy the info," I said, taking another bite out of my wings.

Shaking her head, "I'll be glad if you do, holla. I'm 'bout tired of David assuming we having sex," she rolled her eyes, covering her mouth to belch. Then, teasing, "You think you're over that girl Sabrina," she laughed.

"We going there? Ava, you KNOW I'm over that crazy-ass girl. I can deal with a little crazy but bleaching my clothes and scratching my car is too damn much for me," I shook my head, sickened by the thought of Sabrina Wells.

"Mm-hmm, that was fucked up. I thought she was the one by how close y'all were, living together and shit. Fucked up how things turned out; you were in love too." Ava wiped her mouth, burping again.

Sabrina was a Cadmus Cougar cheerleader. I was the only freshman on the basketball team and starting. After my first championship, she walked up to me and asked for my autograph. She had game, making me feel like a celebrity. I heard a few things about her around campus, so I was reluctant to date her, but after hanging out, I fell hard for her. Sabrina was fly too, 5'7", dark skin, thin waist, fat ass, and thick in all the right places. What I liked most about her was that I could talk to her about anything; she wasn't judgmental and very understanding. My homies still clowned me for being a virgin, but Sabrina didn't. Things were heating up between us, and I knew she was ready to fuck. I can't lie, I was too, but I was also scared as shit! I didn't know what to do; I watched A LOT of porn, but looking at sex and having sex was different.

Sabrina knocked on my door after leaving a fraternity party one Friday night. I opened it; she stumbled in, smelling like alcohol. Her arms were flimsy, she lifted her shirt, and her head got stuck; I helped her take it off. Then, wobbling, Sabrina unbuttoned her pants and stood on her tippy toes, pressing her wet lips against mine. Upset, she managed to get that drunk; I moved my head back, "Kiss me, Christian," Sabrina slurred, "I want you; don't you want me?"

I waved my hand, turning my lips up. I was not too fond of the smell of liquor. Despite the stench, I eyed Sabrina's sexy body, and she instantly turned me on. I kissed her, lifted her by the waist, and wrapped her legs around me. I leaned her against the wall, and she grabbed my head, kissing me deeply. Aroused, I was ready to feel every inch of her. I bolted the door, ensuring my roommate couldn't get in, and carried her to my bed. Sabrina moaned, unbuttoning her bra and exposing her perky full breasts. Wide-eye, I licked my lips, grabbed her breast, squeezed them together, and glided my tongue over her nipples. Her skin was soft and smelled like vanilla. She lifted her body, and I pulled her pants and her underwear off. Completely naked, I slowly kissed her neck, and my tongue made a trail to her stomach. She moaned louder this time. Hoping the porn was good tutorials over the years, I spread her legs, stuck my tongue out, and licked her pussy, gently teasing her clitoris.

"Oh Christian, that feels so good, baby," her hips swayed in circles.

She tasted sweet, I thought as I licked her pussy like ice cream. My lips gripped her healthy clit gently, and I sucked harder. Finally, Sabrina grabbed my head and fed me her pussy. Instinctively, I licked her faster, feeling her pussy get wetter, which drove me crazy; I stopped to grab a condom from the nightstand.

She pulled me closer, "No, we don't need that; just fuck me."

Sabrina let out a moan when I slid inside her. We kissed passionately, and she wrapped her legs around me, forcing me further into her canal. I stroked, imitating the porn I often watched. Then, mesmerized and happy to know I pleased her, I grunted and grabbed her ass; I felt myself about to climax. "Baby, I'm about to cum." I sped up the tempo and felt Sabrina embrace me tighter.

"I'm cumming too, baby," she screamed. "Yes, baby, damn! I love you," she hollered.

Panting, I lay beside her and kissed her lips softly, trying to catch my breath. *I can't believe this is what I've been missing,* I thought. I wrapped my arms around her and cuddled before falling fast asleep.

Sabrina and I moved in together Sophomore year. I trusted her with my secrets; I even thought about marrying her. Her support was unwavering, like my mother's, especially off the court; Sabrina's face was the first one I saw waking up from the anesthesia. Wanting to be a great girlfriend, she stopped cheerleading to sit out the rest of the season and accompanied me to post-op appointments. Rehabilitation was easy with her, and things were great until, Junior year, March Madness. "You should be ready to play," she plopped down on the couch and turned the TV down.

Shaking my head, "I don't know, babe, it's Junior year. I need to get my grades up. Law school is competitive," I grabbed the remote and turned the TV back up, "I need to get accepted."

"That's silly—you played before and had good grades. So, what's the difference now?" She stood in front of the TV with her hands on her waist.

"Baby, I barely hold a 3.5 GPA; that's not good enough. Sabrina, you can go back to cheering. You don't have to sit out because I don't want to play," I grabbed my phone to stream the game.

She sucked her teeth, "Basketball and cheering was our thing together. You said things wouldn't be different, and now you are switching up," she grabbed my phone.

"Don't be dramatic, ain't shit change," we made eye contact, "How 'bout, I'll go to the games and support your fine ass cheering," I grabbed her ass and moved her from in front of the TV.

Sabrina mumbled to herself quietly, "That's not good enough."

"Why it ain't? It should be unless you were with me cause of ball," I smirked.

She chuckled and spoke under her breath, "You just realizing that" she rolled her eyes.

I stood up and towered over her, "What the fuck you say?" Upset that I didn't listen to my homies; she played ME like I played basketball.

"I'm over this. The plan was after you recovered, you'd get back to playing, and I'd cheer," Sabrina shrugged her shoulders, "I should have been left your ass," she walked into the room.

Following behind her, "So you, a lil groupie, thought you could ride this gravy train until the pros? You had me fooled for real, girl," I gritted my teeth.

"I'm moving out, Christian. I'm over this," Sabrina stood in my face pointing and squinting her eyes, "Maybe I was with you because you were the star player. But don't deny being with me benefited you too," she grabbed her clothes and threw them into the suitcase.

I clenched my teeth; she struck a nerve. I opened her drawers and flung her clothes everywhere, "Get all your shit and get the fuck out BITCH!"

"What did you call me?" She stopped packing and looked up at me.

"You heard me; get the fuck on," turning my back, I felt the most brutal punch. It took everything in me not to slap the shit out of her. "Don't get fucked up, Sabrina. Keep your hands to yourself," I walked into the living room and grabbed my keys and phone to leave. I dialed Ava's cell, "Ava are you home? I'm about to pull up on you. Can I kick it there tonight?" She knew how to calm me down, so her place was the best for me.

"Walk out that door, Christian; I swear I'm fucking all your shit up," Sabrina threatened.

"Whatever, girl, I'm tired of your ass. Do whatever," I slammed the door, pissed; I drove fuming. *She had me fooled*, I thought.

"What happened, Bro," Ava read my facial expression and immediately hugged me.

"Sabrina, I can't believe her ass, talking 'bout she with me 'cause she knew I was going pro," I shrugged, "What kind of groupie shit is that?" I pulled my hat down, hiding my face.

Crossing her arms, "People will do whatever if they think you are a meal ticket," she raised her right brow, "Maybe she didn't understand what she was signing up for?"

"What is it to understand? I was straight up with her about my needs and not playing ball," I quickly dismissed Ava's perspective.

She handed me a pop, "What will you do since y'all live together?"

"She is packing her shit, but I don't know where she is going," I opened the can and took a sip.

Ava gave me a half smile, "I never liked her ass anyway," she said, laughing.

"You had me fooled," I chuckled and shook my head, "Females, y'all know how to conceal shit."

"You loved her; what was I to do—tell you I don't like her? She seemed cool but just a bit off to me. I can't explain it; she was doing too much," she pursed her lips.

"Yeah, that shit was all for show," Ava and I talked until her alarm ranged.

"Excuse me," she stepped over me and headed to the bathroom, "It's after 7:00 AM. What time is your first class?" she asked, closing the bathroom door behind her.

I got up from the floor and tossed her pillow on the bed, "I don't have class today, but I have therapy," I turned on my phone. "This chic called my phone ten times and left eight messages," I stared at my cell.

"I know she's hotter than fish grease," Ava walked out of the bathroom and sat on the bed.

"Let me get back to my apartment. I'll call you later," I picked up my hat and zipped my jacket.

"Be careful, Christian," Ava shut the door.

I got closer to my Jeep and saw scratches all over it. *This crazy bitch!* I thought and circled, surveying the damages. Finally, I got into my truck and drove back to my apartment, mad that she had vandalized my shit. This bitch didn't even bother locking my door. Guess I didn't know her like I thought I did; petty ass. The pungent stench of bleach hit my nose as I walked into the apartment. I strolled into the room, and Sabrina tossed my clothes everywhere; my jeans were faded, and my shirts had holes from bleach soaking in them overnight. She ruined everything, including my bed linen.

I picked up my cellphone and dialed her number; she answered on the first ring, "You must've made it home, huh," she laughed.

"What the fuck is your problem? Why did you damage all my shit?" I shouted into the phone.

"That's what you get, Christian. You gone learn about fucking with the wrong BITCH," she screamed and hung up.

I inhaled and called my mother; I didn't have the money to replace my things and needed help, "Hey sweetheart, I'm surprised to hear from you. Did you already go to therapy?" she sounded cheerful.

I sighed slowly, "Nah, Ma, I didn't make it. I can't believe I'm calling you about this, but Sabrina destroyed all of my things. She threw bleach everywhere because I told her I don't plan on playing basketball anymore, then moved out," I sobbed.

"WHAT! Why would she do that? She didn't spend her money buying anything; Sabrina had no business ruining your property," my mom paused a few minutes, "Stop crying, baby, those are just things; I'll send you money to replace it." She exhaled, "I know you don't want to hear this, but I warned you people won't always understand you or your decisions," she sounded concerned.

"I know, Ma; I didn't think she would be one of them," I wiped my eyes. I dreaded talking to Coach Smith, my fans, and the media to avoid reasons like this. "I just really loved her, Ma."

"I know, but love, don't act like that, baby. Trust me. I'm about to head to the bank to put money into your account. Get to therapy and call me later?" she said, hanging up the phone.

The following year was the hardest. First, it took me a while to get over Sabrina. Then, on top of the breakup, I had a lot of disappointed fans after I announced I wouldn't be returning to basketball.

Life was finally feeling normal; it was Senior year, my final semester, and I was happy again. Harrison Law accepted me into their program, and graduation was near. I had met a few girls here and there, but nothing serious. It was hard for me to be vulnerable enough to trust another woman, how I trusted Sabrina.

"I still can't believe you're not playing ball, Christian," Ava took a bite out of her chicken, "I love basketball and can't imagine not playing. When I'm not bouncing a basketball, I think of bouncing one. When I'm not thinking of bouncing the ball, I'm bouncing the ball, but you had to do what made you happiest."

Sipping on my pop, "Yup," I rubbed my stomach stuffed from dinner; I exhaled, "Ready to go? I got a paper to write," I wrapped my arm around Ava, "I got the check," I winked, leaving the restaurant.

I drove home, listening to old-school music, and reflected on the last year of my life. It was such a roller coaster. When life got heavy, or I needed inspiration, I listened to Rev. Paul Jones's *I Won't Complain*. I turned on the song and sang as I drove home.

I pulled into my apartment complex, parked, and cut the engine off. I sat there for 20 minutes listening to music. Over the years, music has become my stress therapy. I finally got out of my Jeep, walked into my apartment, and sat on the sectional. I thought about the beautiful chic I saw earlier as I grabbed the course agenda to see what chapter to read first. I signed up for two summer classes to boost my GPA, hoping to earn a 3.8 GPA.

Two weeks into the fall semester, Ava and I managed not to bump into the girlie I saw leaving her dorm. The campus was big, but damnit, it can't be this big. She did me a solid and walked the floors introducing herself as RA, and she didn't see anyone who matched the description I gave her. After failed attempts, mixed with being bombarded with other student-athletes trying to holler at her, Ava called it quits on our mission.

Defeated, I decided to leave it alone and focus on classes; they were already whooping my ass. I spent hours in the main library writing my paper, and my eyes were growing heavy. I packed my bag to head home, and finally shawty walked into the library with a friend. They were deep in conversation, not noticing me. My stomach dropped. I didn't want to interrupt their conversation, but I had to say something to her. Her friend accidently bumped into the unknown lady, and her phone dropped out of her hand. I seized the opportunity to make a move.

"Here you go, pretty lady," I reached for her phone and wiped it off, handing it back to her, "Looks like you were lucky it didn't break."

She looked up at me, smiled, and softly grabbed the phone. Then, with the sweetest voice, she said, "Thank you."

I winked, "No worries. I'm Christian Powell," I held my hand out and introduced myself to her and her friend, whose mouth was wide open.

"She's Essence, and I'm Madison," her friend grabbed my hand first.

I shook her hand and let it go, then grabbed Essence's hand. "Nice to meet you, Essence. I see you both aren't the typical freshman that never visits the library," I said, immediately hating that I sounded so corny.

Her friend Madison wrinkled her brows, "What makes you think we are freshmen?"

"For starters, I think I would have met you two beautiful ladies before today," I directed my attention to Essence, "I'm a senior; we would have bumped into each other years ago," I glanced back at Madison.

"We could have transferred," Madison crossed her arms and pursed her lips.

Essence rolled her eyes at Madison, "We're freshmen," she lightly shoved her friend, "My coach prefers that I study in the library."

I narrowed my eyes, "What sport do you play? I noticed you moved into the athletic dorm," I eagerly awaited her response.

"Track and field; I run the 100-meter dash and the 200," she looked up and smiled.

"Wow, so you're fast, huh? I have to check you out. Do you play sports too, Madison?" she looked impatient, glancing at her phone.

"No, she doesn't play any sports," Essence answered for her friend, who clearly looked disengaged, "Do you play any sports, Christian?"

"No, I just go to school and work." I omitted I was a former basketball star; I hoped she didn't recognize me from any articles or sports coverage.

"Oh, I didn't want to assume you played anything since you are so tall," squinting her eyes, "How tall are you, by the way?"

"Six feet, six inches," I smiled.

"OMG! I thought you were 6'4," Essence giggled.

"It's ok. Maybe I can study with you one of these days since your coach wants you to study in the library?" I strayed from the subject.

"That will be fine. I could use some study partners, and since you're a senior, I'm sure you can show me some of your study techniques," she flirted.

"Have you decided on your major yet? I know it's early, but picking a major is major, you know," I laughed.

She grinned and looked at the ground, fidgeting, "Honestly, I haven't. I want to meet with my advisor to discuss lucrative careers before selecting a major."

"Great idea," I threw my head back, "I wished I thought of that," I put my hands into my jacket pocket, "I chose criminal law."

Her eyes twinkled. "Really, My father's an attorney. He used to go to college here—Franklin Donaldson."

I leaned forward, "The football player? Wow! I heard about him. He's one of the reasons I wanted to become an attorney; his story was inspirational," I smiled, "I know he is making big money representing those famous clients," I joked.

Essence laughed, "He does alright."

Reaching for my phone, "Would you like to exchange numbers? I figured we gotta keep in touch if we study sometime," I handed it to her to save her contact information.

"Of course," she smiled and programmed her number, "How else will you reach me?" Essence smirked and gave me her phone to do the same, "Save your number."

Handing her back her phone, "I'll let y'all get to studying. It's late; I've already interrupted too much of your study time," I placed my phone back into my pocket.

"It was nice meeting you," Essence said and walked away.

"Likewise," I turned to watch them stroll into the library. I got into my Jeep, turned my music up high, and headed home excited to have met the girl who's crowded my thoughts since I laid eyes on her.

Chapter Three

ESSENCE

"So, that's the guy you told me about?" Madison probed, sitting across the study table, "If so, good Lord, he is extra fine."

I grinned, "Girl, yes! So that was him," I smiled from ear to ear, "Hopefully, we can study soon," I opened my book and bit my pen.

"I didn't want to be all in the conversation; I sensed he was interested in you, so I walked away, but damn boo, a senior?" Madison opened her book and grabbed a highlighter and pen to take notes.

"Yup, I hope he's a good guy. I can't deal with another liar," I highlighted a page and jotted some notes.

She pursed her lips. "Mm-hmm, all you can do is take your time if you're interested." Then, Madison looked up from her book, "If you asked me, I say stick to these books and track; maybe study with him here and there, but you don't want to get all lost into somebody your freshman year; there's so much to do and people to meet on this campus," she appeared concerned. Finally, nudging me, "Why you ain't say he favored that one rapper, Classic Man?" her eyes narrowed.

"Jidenna!" I chuckled. "He does favor him, just extra tall and a body that looks sculpted from clay."

"Girl, yes," Madison high-fived me, "Just don't get caught up; he's way too fine to be single," she twisted her mouth.

I exhaled slowly, "Yeah, you're probably right," I turned the page quickly, dismissing the conversation, "Are you going to come to the track meet next Saturday? It's our rivalry competition."

She squinted her eyes, "Saturday, I'll be home, Jhace is visiting from Kentucky, and we plan on chilling; you know I miss my baby," Madison pouted.

I cracked a slight smile, "That's cool, my parents will be here, but next time girl, you better come see me run," I pointed my finger in her face.

We stayed in the library for the next two hours, then left for our separate dorms. Madison conveniently lived across the street from the main library, so we hung out whenever I was in her neck of the woods. My roommate was a sophomore and was hardly in the room, and unlike first-year students, she didn't have a curfew which was a perfect for me. I took advantage of being alone every chance I got. I set my bookbag on the bed and grabbed my phone to check my text messages.

I scrolled and saw that I had received a message from Christian: *Were you still studying Beautiful?*

I blushed and put my phone down, unsure of what I wanted to say. I didn't expect Christian to text so soon, but I was glad he did.

I replied: *Yes, I just got in from the library. What are you doing?* and plugged my phone into the charger; I had 10 percent battery left. I undressed and stared anxiously at my phone, seeming like forever before Christian responded back.

He texted back: *That's good. I've been at home watching Sports Center. I need to start studying for an exam that I have on Thursday.*

I added exclamation marks to stress the urgency: *That's just two days away; get to it!!!*

Christian texted: *I will; I wanted to say good night before I did.* He added a smiley face emoji.

I smiled: *That's sweet and considerate of you. Good night then* I sent a smirking emoji.

The following two hours, I was up, I had a full day of classes and practice afterward, but I was restless. My thoughts were everywhere, my upcoming exam, the track meet, and Christian. I shut my eyes and tossed for the next few minutes. Then, feeling overwhelmed, I grabbed the medicine bottle and swallowed the rectangle pill without water. Since prom, I have developed anxiety and have been taking prescription pills to manage it.

The morning was here before I knew it; I reached for my cell phone, turned on one of my favorite songs, *Closer* by Goapele and sang along. I got out of bed, grabbed my favorite distressed jeans and a pink polo, and threw it on the bed; swaying my hips, I twirled, "Closer to my dreams," I sang out, feeling energized despite the lack of sleep. I knocked on the bathroom to make sure my suitemate wasn't there, and I walked in and locked the door when I didn't get a response.

Steamed filled the bathroom, I held my hand under the water, checked the temperature, and stepped inside. I lathered my body, which was completely white with soapsuds, stood underneath the water, rinsing the bubbles from my naked body, and grabbed the shampoo. I planned on air-drying my curls since they always looked fuller that way.

I finished showering and wiped the mist from the glass to see my reflection. Then, I held my toothbrush like a microphone and sang to the next song playing from the other room. Mid-song, I brushed my teeth, wrapped a towel around my head, and walked back into my room, sitting on the bed.

I grabbed my phone and read the latest message from Christian: *I was having breakfast with my friend Ava. If you're awake, would you like to join us?*

My stomach grumbled, smiling, breakfast sounds nice. I sent a quick text back: *I'll be down in a few, and I'll see you there.*

When I finished putting on lotion and doing my hair, the scent of lavender, vanilla, and Jojoba filled the room. I grabbed a matching panty and bra set, then walked to my full-length mirror to admire my reflection, twisting around to see my firm ass. *Damn,* I thought. I didn't want to be late; I jumped, pulling my pants over my ass. It felt like I was exercising, getting the fitted jeans over it. Finally, I slid on my Nike Air Force flip-flops and read the incoming text from Christian: *I'm here.*

I sent the text and headed to the café: *I'm on my way down now.* My stomach rumbled even louder as I approached the cafeteria. Christian stuck out like a sore thumb towering over everyone. He looked good in camo pants, a blue chambray shirt, retro Nike Jordans, and a backward-fitted cap.

I walked up behind him, tapping him on the shoulder, "Hey there," I filled my glass with orange juice.

He turned around, looked down, and gave me a half hug so he didn't drop his tray, "Hey Essence," he looked at me smiling, "Did you sleep well?"

Nodding my head, "I slept well when I finally got to sleep," I giggled, "Running track and classes can drain me, that you'd think I would hit the bed exhausted. But I tossed and turned until I finally dozed off."

Looking at his watch, "I'm surprised you're awake," he raised his right brow.

"Yeah, I'm not tired; where is your friend?" I turned my head, observing the room as if I knew how Ava looked.

"Ava will be down in a second. She's an R.A. here, and a student had an issue. But unfortunately, I was too hungry to wait," he smiled, rubbing his belly.

I laughed, "I'm hungry too. Did you want to sit close to the door so Ava can see us when she walks in?" I suggested grabbing a plate full of hot cakes and sausage.

"Mm-huh, that's a good idea," Christian led the way to the table. He put his tray down and walked around the table to pull out a seat for me.

Taking a seat, I thought, *he's such a gentleman.*

He waved his hand at the door, "There she is," he stood up, "Let me introduce you to her—she's mad cool," he smiled.

Ava scanned her badge and headed towards our table. Her smile stretched ear to ear, revealing her pearly white teeth. She was tall, athletic, at least 5'10", with brown skin and grey eyes; she wore her hair in a bob and full lips. She was beautiful; it was hard to believe they were only friends. Christian wrapped his arms around her, and I eyed them closely, peeping their chemistry.

"Hey Chris, you look nice today," she complimented him and turned to introduce herself, "Hi, I'm Ava," extending her hand, "Christian has filled my ears about you."

I stood up and shook her hand, "Really? What did he say?" I furrowed my brows.

Smiling, she looked at Christian, who was shaking his head, "Nothing major," she chuckled.

He interrupted, "I just said you were beautiful," eyeing his plate of food, "I didn't know how long you were going to be, so we both grabbed our food."

"Boy, you hardly wait to eat; I'm about to fix a Belgian waffle" she walked away to grab a tray.

"Now Ava, she can eat," Christian chuckled, eating a bite of his food.

I cut my pancakes into squares, "How long have you two known each other?" I poured syrup, fishing for information.

He counted his fingers. "Shoot; I was ten years old when I met you, Ava, right?" He looked at her as she sat her tray down.

"That's right," Ava eyed Christian and placed her hand on his shoulder, "I forgot to grab something. Can you come with me for a second, please? Is that alright?" she turned to me.

Damn, that shit was rude. I wanted to say, "Hell no," but nodding my head, I decided against it, "Yes, that's fine," I took a bite out of my pancakes.

I watched the two of them walk away. Christian put his arm around Ava's shoulder and leaned his ear to hear what Ava was saying. *I wonder what the hell was so important,* I thought. They returned to the table five minutes later. I ate most of my pancakes and almost finished eating my sausage. Christian sat back down, looking everywhere but at his food, appearing distracted. Whatever she said to him plainly had his attention divided. There was a level of awkwardness at the table, and I felt out of place.

I looked down at my watch, "Wow, I just remembered I have class in about 40 minutes," I lied, standing up to get my tray. I had three hours to burn before I had to get to Accounting 101, but I couldn't stand sitting at the table for another moment with the two of them, not knowing what I had witnessed. The weirdness was an even bigger sign that I should continue focusing on school and track and leave dudes alone; I didn't need any drama.

Christian got up from the table and walked over to me, "Let me carry that tray for you and walk you out." We walked to the trash, and he placed the tray on the rack and wrapped his arms around me, "Is it alright to text you later? I'm sorry about breakfast. It didn't go as I anticipated it would," he looked sincere as he waited for my answer.

Shifting my weight from side to side, I said, "Man, I don't know." I wrinkled my brows, "I don't want to be stepping on anybody's toes."

Christian laughed, exposing the deepest dimple; he tilted his head back, "Toes? Essence, you not hardly stepping on anybody's toes." He squeezed my shoulder.

"Are you sure? Because it didn't look that way to me earlier," I played in my hair.

"I'm positive, Essence. Ava has a boyfriend. She wanted to converse about something important, that's all," he said reassuringly, "She picked the wrong time, though," he gave a half smile.

I bit my bottom lip and raised my eyebrow, "I don't know, Christian," I said, looking down at the floor.

Christian placed his hand under my chin and lifted my head, "Please, Essence?" he held up praying hands.

I hummed, pretending to think about it, "Yes, Christian...you can call me." I laughed.

"Yes," he reached down to give me a tight hug, "Now gone before you're late for class," he said playfully.

I giggled, placing my hand over my mouth, "Shut up, bye," I walked toward the elevators and pressed the button to go upstairs. As I waited, I wondered what Ava said to Christian, which seemed to have shaken him up. I wasn't going to harp on it, but one thing was for sure—I wouldn't end up looking like a fool again.

Chapter Four

CHRISTIAN

I sat down with Ava, "You telling me you couldn't wait to call me later to talk to me about that?" I was so heated she almost jeopardized my getting to know Essence further.

She pursed her lips, "Nope." Ava rolled her eyes, she was a savage, and at times I didn't know if she was looking out for me or didn't want to share me. Ava could be possessive at times. "I'm trying to have your back, Christian, because when you get hurt, I'm the first person you come calling," she took a bite of her bacon, "Make sure you know what you are doing, this time, before getting deep with her," she looked at me. Then, she picked up her cup and gulped down her apple juice.

I placed my palm against my forehead, "I appreciate you having my back," I took a sip of juice, "But I damn near had to convince shawty we weren't kicking it," I took off my cap and ran my fingers over my waves. Someone interrupted my thoughts as they shouted, "What's up, Chris!" Unsure who it was that said it, I threw my fist in the air, "What up, doe," and acknowledged the stranger.

Ava waved her hands at a few students that walked past our table, "Christian, I didn't mean to come off like we were together; that was not my intention," she stood up from the table, "If I see her, I'll let her know we ain't kicking it," Ava bumped her hip against me.

Waving my hand, "No, don't go trying to fix nothing. I got it, but thank you for apologizing," I grabbed my phone, vibrating against my leg, and squinted my eyes, puzzled by the unknown 313 number. "Ava, I'll catch up to you later; I got to take this call."

I got up from the table and walked out of the cafeteria to better hear the caller on the other end, "Hello, is this Christian Powell?" The unidentified caller asked.

"Yes, it's me—who is this?" I crumpled my brows, wondering who was on the other end.

"Christian, my name is Lieutenant Carl Watson from the Redford Police station; we need to talk; is this a good time, son?" He had a warm tone.

"Uh, yes," I hesitated, "May I ask what the matter involves?"

"Son, it's imperative that you come to the station immediately. Do you think that you can come in today?" he paused.

"I have a class within the next 30 minutes," I looked at my watch.

"Is it possible you can skip? It's an urgent matter," he pressed.

I stuttered, "Can you tell me any information now?"

"No, Christian, we need to speak in person. Can you get to the precinct today?" Lieutenant Watson was stern this time.

I exhaled, and I waited for a long moment. My thoughts swirled.

"Hello, are you there?" he asked.

"Yes, I'm here; sure, I can get there. It'll take me about two hours; I'm in East Lansing," I said, hoping the lieutenant would give me a hint to ease my mind.

"That's fine; I'll be waiting. Do you need directions, son?" he cleared his throat.

"I can G.P.S. myself," I said, slightly troubled.

"We will see you soon then, son," he hung up.

Ava caught up to me outside the cafeteria; I placed the phone back into my pocket and looked up, "Everything okay?" She looked concerned.

I frowned and scratched my head, "I just got a call from the Redford Police Department. A Lieutenant Watson wants me to speak to him in person."

She narrowed her eyes, "Why is a police officer calling you?"

Shrugging my shoulders, "I don't know, but I tell you one thing; if it has something to do with Sabrina, I swear, man." My stomach was in knots; I grabbed my keys from my jacket.

"You better go," Ava tilted her head towards the exit, "I would ride with you, but I have class in 20 minutes."

"You good." I hugged Ava, headed out the door, and called my mom. The phone went straight to the voicemail, "Mom Dukes, I got a call from the Redford police. Can you meet me at the station in an hour?" I hung up and jumped into the Jeep.

I was halfway home and still hadn't heard from my mom. I picked up the phone and called her again, wondering where she could be. I gritted my teeth when I got the voicemail again. *What in the world,* I thought. I redialed the number, and the phone rang three times before returning to voicemail, "Ma, call me, please— it's urgent."

Worried, I pressed the accelerator and looked at the dash. I was going 85 miles an hour down the 96 freeway. My mind wandered all over as I gripped the steering wheel, clenching my jaw. I was almost to the station but decided to exit to stop at my home first. My cell phone rang, and my heart thumped faster, hoping it was my mother, but it was my neighbor.

I answered, my heart in my throat, "Christian, this is Ms. Judy, your neighbor," she sobbed as her voice cracked, "I'm sorry to call and tell you this, but your mother passed away this morning, baby," she cried.

Without a word, I dropped the phone, hit the gas, and swerved onto my street. I felt nauseated. The closer I got, I saw the coroner roll the gurney into the van and police cars parked along the road, and yellow caution tape, that the officers hung from the porch railing. I opened the door, vomited, and ran towards the house past three officers who gathered on the sidewalk.

"Sir, you can't go inside," an officer called out and grabbed my arm, stopping me in my tracks.

"I live here; what do you mean I can't go in there?" I sobbed, "What happened to my momma?" I snatched my arm and ran up the pavement to the porch.

"Hello, I am Officer James Tolbert from the Redford Police Department," the officer placed his hand on my shoulder and gripped it firmly, "Did our lieutenant call you?"

My eyes filled with tears, and I felt a tingling sensation over my body as the officer explained that a home invasion had occurred. Astonished by the news, "What happened?" I mumbled, my lips trembling. I looked across the yard over to Ms. Judy, holding a tissue in her hands and wiping away her tears.

"I found her," she yelled, walking over to me.

"Ma'am, please allow me to speak to this gentleman privately," Office Tolbert turned back and continued to explain.

"No, she can stay; continue telling me," I stepped off the porch, walked over to my neighbor, my mother's best friend, and wrapped my arms around her.

"We received a 911 call reporting shots fired in the midnight hours. Arriving on the scene, we approached the home, saw the door ajar, and walked in and found the victim, your mother shot," the officer grabbed his notepad and asked for a few statements.

I felt my knees giving out, and I dropped to the ground. I ran my fingers through the grass, pulling it from the roots. "I can't lose my momma. I don't have nobody—what am I going to do?" I said, weeping.

"Your mother has been staying with me, but she said she hadn't heard of any crimes lately and decided to stay home," Ms. Judy wiped her nose and continued to talk, "I wish she would have stayed," she said, placing her hands on my back and rubbing me softly. "Get up, baby. You have to be strong. I know it's hard, but we will get through this."

Officer Tolbert walked down from the porch, "My condolences; we will be in touch," he handed me his card.

"I should have called you sooner," Ms. Judy wept.

Hyperventilating, trying to catch my breath, "I received a call from Lieutenant Watson, but I didn't imagine this," my chest rose and repeatedly fell, "I can't believe I lost my momma," I stood up.

"Hush, baby, try to catch your breath," Ms. Judy reached into her jacket pocket and gave me a tissue.

After the officers cleared the scene, I walked into the house and sat on the sofa. I picked up a picture of my mother from the coffee table and stared at it. Tears flowed down my face; I shook my head. She didn't deserve this. I walked around the house to observe if the intruders had stolen anything. The smell of her white diamonds perfume lingered in the air and gave me a feeling she was still there. What was once a perfect feeling of being home was now filled with anger and grief.

I barely got through the next few days. If it weren't for Ava and Ms. Judy, I don't know how I would have planned the funeral. I even shared the bad news with Essence, who immediately offered her support and attended the funeral, which made me happy. However, I hesitated to call her. I didn't want her to feel overwhelmed or obligated to be there for me.

The funeral was over, and I sat in the Church's family center and listened to my mother's friends chat about her; they loved her just as much as I did. Hearing the stories about my mom gave me a sense of calmness.

"Hey, you okay?" Ava tapped my shoulder, breaking my reverie, "Did you get a chance to eat?" She stood up and eyed me.

"No, but I'm good—just a bit exhausted," I looked down at my watch.

"You need to eat something, Christian. I'll be right back," she walked into the kitchen area and returned with a plate full of food minutes later. "Eat some of this," she said, putting the plate of chicken, macaroni, greens, yams, and ham in front of me.

I poked at it with my fork and finally took a bite of the mac and cheese; it was rich and cheesy, and I scarfed it down in one bite.

Ava shoved me gently, "Glad to see you eating," she kidded and exhaled slowly, "The funeral was nice. I was surprised to see Essence. Y'all look pretty close." She changed the subject.

"It was nice, wasn't it?" I wiped my mouth, "Essence, and I got a little closer."

"I take it you talked to her about everything, right," she asked, concerned.

"Yeah, we talked," I got up from the table to throw away my plate and stared at the clock on the wall; I was anxious to leave the repass, "I have to study and make up a few papers I missed, let's head out," I got up to say my goodbyes to everybody.

You could say I made it to campus on a wing and a prayer; my eyes rolled shut a few times as I drove back. A bolt of energy ran through my body when I saw Essence calling. I don't know why she has this effect on me. It would be best to proceed with caution, but I craved Essence with such a desire I'd do anything to have her. I should be running, but everything in me wanted Essence like I needed my next breath.

"Hey," I answered the phone. I was sure Essence heard the smile in my voice.

"Hey Christian, I wanted to see how you were doing. Your mother's homegoing was nice," her voice was sincere.

I inhaled and exhaled slowly, "I'm good, considering the circumstances. I appreciate you being there for me."

"It was the least I could do. If you need someone to talk to, you can always call me. What are you up to?" Essence lingered, "Are you driving?" her voice inflected.

"Yes, I'm driving back to East Lansing—what about you?" I hoped she called, wanting to see me. Dating was difficult because everyone complicated it. I admit going with the flow was never my strong suit, and the few women I dated thought I was too good to be true; being athletic and faithful was unheard of.

Essence sighed, "I am at the library studying for an accounting exam. We should study soon."

I smiled, "I'm down with that. I can make it to you in 30 minutes; just let me grab us some coffee," I offered.

"Seriously?" she asked cheerfully, "I wasn't talking about today."

"Yeah, I know, but I need to study," I chuckled, "I can be there in a few. I'm exiting the freeway now," I approached the light at Harrison Road.

"Alright then; I'm on the second floor, the north side of the library," she said, hanging up.

I grabbed a caramel macchiato and headed to the library; my adrenalin was pumping. The elevator doors opened, and I walked the floor until I saw Essence's head buried in her book, with a yellow highlighter gliding across the page. I cleared my throat as I approached the table.

We made eye contact, and she smiled and stood up, wrapping her arms around me. She inhaled deeply, "You smell good," she let go of my embrace, looked up, and grinned.

I sat the coffees down, "Thank you, and so do you," I handed her a cup and sat down at the table.

Essence took a sip of coffee, "What are you wearing?"

"Armani cologne," I unclipped my bookbag and took out my law book. I tried keeping my cool, but I giggled when I caught her looking at me smiling. "What?" I grinned.

"I'm glad you're here," she rested her head on her hands.

"Word?" I looked around, "I imagine dudes try to holla at you all the time. How many of them hollered at you tonight?" I teased.

Essence threw her head back, "None!" She pursed her lips.

We both laughed and locked eyes again. I grabbed Essence's hand, rubbed my thumb across her knuckles, and then pressed my lips against it. I held her hand a little longer and proceeded to study. We lost track of time researching and enjoying each other's presence, I glanced at my watch, and 1:00 AM was approaching. Pretending to be engrossed in my book, I watched Essence part her lips as she read; damn, she even made reading look good. Her lips looked so soft. I envisioned how it feels to make love to her. I shook my head and attempted to get the thoughts out of my mind. I looked back at Essence, who was smiling.

"Wow, it's late," she looked at her phone and yarned, "I'm getting tired, are you?"

Nodding, "Yeah, we should get going," I was disappointed I couldn't spend more time with her.

She gathered her books and placed them into her bookbag, "The last bus ran at midnight; I'm going to walk to Madison's since she lives across the street from the library," she dialed her number.

"I can take you home. You ain't gotta walk; somebody might snatch you up," I placed my hand on Essence's shoulder, "I'm sure your girl is knocked out anyway," I snickered.

"Boy, ain't nobody gone kidnap me," she chuckled.

"I would," I blurted out and immediately grinned.

In a flirtatious tone, "You wouldn't have to, Christian. I'd go wherever you'd take me," Essence said and winked.

I played it smooth, but Essence turned me on, "Let me start with taking you home then." I grabbed her hand and walked her to my Jeep.

We arrived at her dorm, and she invited me up. I didn't know what to think; I rubbed my clammy hands on my pants. I tried playing it cool. My heart pounded against my chest as I followed behind her. I stood inches away from her and saw goose bumps form on her neck. As I breathed, she turned her key, opened the door, and flipped on the light switch.

"Thank you for bringing me home," she turned and held the door blocking the entry.

I didn't want to pressure her to invite me in, "You're welcome, boo," I said calmly. I leaned forward, wrapped my arm around her waist, and walked away. My palm hit my forehead, "Before I forget, Saturday, clear your schedule—I'm taking you out," I flashed a smile.

She raised her brow, "Just like that, huh?" Essence smiled and placed her right hand on her hip.

"Yup, just like that, can't let you be alone on Valentine's Day," I laughed, grabbing her hand and interlocking our fingers, "I'm about to get up out of here and let you get to sleep," I pulled her closer and leaned down to kiss her on the cheek. "Good night, Beautiful," I said, stepping back from the door and getting one good look at her before she closed the door. *Saturday, hurry up*, I thought.

Essence opened the door and peeped her head out, "See ya'," she chuckled.

It felt like a month of Sundays passed by the time the end of the week rolled around. Wanting to impress her, I planned our date to the last detail, hoping she'd enjoy it. We talked daily; I learned a few things about her that I wanted to incorporate into the activities. Finally, Saturday arrived, and the weather was nice for a February night. I pulled up to her dorm, squirted some breath spray, and checked myself in the rearview mirror. Tiger lilies were her favorite; I grabbed them from the back seat and headed to her room. A few chics I passed in the hallway "Oohed and aahed," with approval. I smiled from their validation. My eyes widened when the door swung open, "Dang, you must have a sixth sense; I didn't even knock!" I teased.

Essence gasped as her eyes focused on the flowers, "Oh my God, these are my favorite," she reached for the tiger lilies, sniffed them, and placed them on the dresser. Then, she embraced me tightly, "Thank you, thank you, thank you!" she smiled.

I spun her around to check out her outfit; she wore a red sweater, jeans that hugged her hips perfectly, and Ugg boots with bows on the back. I wore slim-fit jeans, a striped top, and Gucci loafers.

"You're welcome, baby; I'm glad you like them," I smiled and hugged her again. It felt good, feeling her body against mine. We lingered for a while, and we parted, "You look good, Essence," I skimmed her up and down.

"Same to you. I see we complement each other," Essence touched my arm, "Are you going to tell me where you are taking me?"

I nodded, "It's a surprise, but I promise you'll like it," I looked at my watch, "We have to get going."

Essence sprayed herself with a sexy scent that followed her as we headed to the Jeep. We held hands while listening to, *Earned It (Fifty Shades of Grey)* by The Weekend. Before long, we pulled into the parking lot, "What is this place," she held my hand tighter, walking into the venue.

"It's a poetry slam," I grinned, opening the door to let her walk in. The hostess sat us in the reserved booth just before the host introduced the next poet. We clapped and gave the waitress our order. She returned with some finger foods and drinks. We enjoyed our appetizers, and as the evening passed, the host announced it was time for open mic. Nervous, I patted the sweat off my forehead and gulped down some pop. I wrote often but have yet to perform. Essence loved poetry, and I wanted to blow her away. I slid out of the booth and walked toward the stage. I gave the host my name, and then he introduced me. I cleared my throat and took a deep breath. The lights were bright; I squinted and made eye contact with Essence as I recited,

"How can we get past this? Shyness, no words spoken, silence. I want you, but I'm not sure your heart is there. Should I tell you exactly how I feel—are my actions unclear? I reach out to touch you but pull back because of fear. Rejection. Everybody experiences it a time or two, but the reverberated thoughts forces me to draw back from you. Acting out of character and playing different roles as if that'll make you notice me when usually I'm playing Frank. Why hold back how you really feel when you only have one life to live, and you know what they say, 'Closed mouths don't get fed.' So, with that said, if you allow me, I can be your biggest fan. You can have me, the best of three—I can be your homie, your lover, and your friend. We can recite poetry, have dialect or shit—we can make love from dusk until the sun sets. Stop me from being too direct. I just want you to know that I want you."

The audience stood up and gave a round of applause. I took a bow and looked back at Essence, who held her hand over her mouth. The host shook my hand and requested the audience to give me another round of applause as I exited the stage. I approached the booth, and she dove into my arms, "Did you like your surprise?"

"You were amazing! I didn't know you wrote poetry. Why didn't you tell me?" She shoved me gently, we slid back in the booth, and I wrapped my arm around her shoulder.

"I wanted to surprise you," I smiled, "You told me you liked poetry, and I thought it would be different to take you somewhere and, possibly, do something that no one has done for you before," I grinned at my execution. I leaned in and pressed my lips against hers; our lips parted, and our tongues glided each other's, and I grabbed the nape of Essence's neck, kissing her deeper. I didn't care who watched.

"Looks like big man gone get him some tonight," shouted someone in the audience. Essence and I stopped and laughed immediately. She wiped her thumb across the bottom of my lip and leaned against my shoulder as we sat and watched the following artists.

"I don't know about you, but I'm starving," I patted my stomach, "You have an appetite?"

Essence nodded in agreement. Finally, we left the venue and drove to Lucy's Lobster, her favorite restaurant. I wasn't a seafood person since I was allergic to shellfish, but I ordered a steak meal. She ordered an endless shrimp dinner we both ate and talked about the event. We were the last guest in the restaurant, and I wanted the evening to continue.

"I guess we should leave," I noticed the waiters were cleaning up. "I don't want to say goodnight to you yet," I admitted.

"Then don't," Essence grabbed my hand as we exited the restaurant.

We listened to D'Angelo's *Brown Sugar* album on the way back to my apartment. In a low tone, I sang the lyrics *Lady* and laid my hand on her lap, rubbing her legs gently. I gazed at Essence, who bit her bottom lip and stared back at me. We walked into my place, and I took her coat and hung it in the closet. Essence made herself comfortable, walked around, and looked at the portraits on the wall. I turned on the vintage record player and played the rest of D'Angelo's album. She stopped, stared at the high school graduation photo of my mother and me, and paused. She continued to explore; walking over to the bookcase, Essence ran her fingers across the spine of the books and squinted a little to read the titles. She sat on the sectional and picked up a frame, "I thought you said you didn't play sports?" She stared at a picture taken of me at the championship game.

I took the picture from her. "I don't anymore," I placed the frame on the table, "Would you like something to drink? I have water, cherry apple juice, and lemonade," I turned my head to look in her direction.

She stood up. "The endless shrimp still has me stuffed, but can you point me toward your bathroom."

"Sure." I pointed toward the bathroom and waited until she walked away before I fluffed the pillows, lit a few scented candles, and dimmed the lights. Essence returned, and her expression immediately changed when she saw the ambiance. She looked down; I could tell she was nervous. Eventually, she sat on the furthest end of the sofa.

Essence inhaled and let out a long sigh, "I have to tell you something."

I scooted closer and grabbed her hand. "You can tell me anything; what's up?" I was anxious to know what was on her mind.

She rested her chin on her hand, "You need to know this," she looked away; I grabbed her chin and turned her head towards me, "I'm...um," she hesitated.

I leaned closer. "There's nothing you can't tell me, Essence." I squeezed her hand gently.

She blurted out, "I never had sex before," she paused and exhaled, "I want to wait until I'm married. I hope you understand," she looked into my eyes and waited.

I let out a sigh of relief. "Baby, you don't have to do anything you don't want to do, and sex is the furthest from my mind, don't get me wrong, I'd love to, but I understand," I grinned and let out a sigh of relief, "I like the fact that you're going to make me wait until we're married before I can have it anyhow," I teased.

Essence burst out in laughter, "Who said I'm marrying you?" She slanted her head and ginned more, "But I do love your confidence."

I chuckled and got up from the couch, "Dance with me," I grabbed her hand and pulled her closer. Essence and I stood in the center of the living room and rocked slowly to the music.

We danced and talked until the sun's rays peered through the blinds. Then, finally, she yawned, "I am so tired. I can't believe we sat up all night."

"Time flies when you're having fun. Of course, that was so cliche, but you get what I mean," I chuckled.

"Guess your smoothness fades after midnight," she teased, laying her head on my chest and closing her eyes.

As she slept, I watched her. I wish I had gotten to know her sooner; my mother would have loved her. The more I was around Essence, the more I fell for her. She was a freshman and had her whole college years to look forward to, and I was graduating. Taking it slow was best, but I couldn't help but envision being with her and wondering if she could be my wife; I was willing to do whatever it took to get us there. I closed my eyes and fell asleep with her in my arms.

Chapter Five

ESSENCE

Christian and I have been inseparable since Valentine's Day. I loved spending time with him; having a boyfriend again was exciting. His temperament was nothing like I'd experienced before. He knew the right words to say, was patient, loving, and kind, and his level of consideration was unmatched; he reminded me a little of my father. I feel guilty, though; the more I spent time with Christian, the less I saw Madison, and I knew that was upsetting for her. She fluently spoke sarcasm and was in rare form the last time we spoke, saying, "When you see Essence, you see Christian, and when you see Christian, you see Essence," she was right. To make it worse, summer was nearing, and we barely saw each other.

Christian landed an internship at my father's law firm, and it was our first weekend apart. I introduced him to my parents, and daddy approved of him after he learned Christian was going into criminal law. Wanting to make up lost time, I decided to spend the weekend with Madison and catch up. My heart was in my throat when I picked up the phone to dial her number; it's been two months since we hung out, and our conversations hadn't been the best lately since she felt I had abandoned our friendship. The phone rang twice, and just as I was hanging up, Madison answered, "Look what the cat dragged in," she scoffed.

I rolled my eyes, "Stop it!" I hated when I felt chastised even if her statement was valid. I dropped the ball several times when she called, wanting to hang out. It was silly of me to assume she'd understand because she was still in a relationship with Jhace, "You got five minutes — let me have it," I sat, arms crossed.

"We good girl," Madison giggled, "Glad to know you're not dead."

"Mm-hmm, what do you have up for the day?" I quickly changed the subject of my absence and focused on the task at hand.

"Nothing, hanging out around the house. What are you and Christian doing?" she teased.

I pursed my lips, "Nothing, I wanted to hang out with you," I paused and waited to see what clever comeback she had, "It's been a while since we hung on the Isle," I smiled; Madison and I loved cruising around the Isle summers before college.

She perked up, "It has been forever," Madison chuckled, "I need to get out of this house. My momma has been riding my nerves, and this single life is for the birds. I swear I gained 15 pounds sitting around eating ice cream," Madison added.

I tilted my head and narrowed my eyes, "Wait, you and Jhace broke up?" I felt terrible; this was the first I'd heard of this. The distance between us was evident, and it grew, "Get dressed; we can talk about it on the way there."

I pulled up to Madison's and put my shades on. It was 95 degrees, sun beaming, and hot enough to fry eggs on the cement. Daddy let me drive his red Corvette convertible. It was my favorite car because I loved how my hair flowed in the wind. I pressed my hand on the horn and smiled when I saw Madison.

"Hey, girl, hey!" She opened the door, hopped in, wrapped her arms around me, and kissed my cheek, "I missed you, girl," our embrace lingered.

"I missed you too," I let go and sucked my teeth, "And you are working that outfit," I pursed my lips.

"Thanks, girl," Madison tugged on the bottom of her skirt, "So, let's roll out — I'm ready for this milkshake to bring the boys to the yard," we chuckled at the Kelis reference. Madison adjusted her full breasts that practically poured out her bra.

She was witty, and her humor was always on point, one of the things I loved about her most. I pulled off and played Juvenile's *Back that azz up*. We danced in our seats, rapping the lyrics. Madison reached over and turned the music down. "On the topic of backing that ass up, you still a virgin?" She twisted her mouth, "Y'all been spending a lot of time together, so spill the tea. Are y'all having sex?" Madison faced me and curled her lip.

My eyes widened, surprised by her directness, "No girl, we not having sex. I told you I was waiting until I got married, remember? Ain't nothing changed," I looked at Madison, whose lips twisted more.

"I don't believe that! So, you are telling me his fine ass is still waiting?" She raised her brow, "I don't know if I could keep my coochie in my pants that long. No disrespect," she said, shaking her head.

"Well, believe it or not, Christian isn't like that. He knows I want to wait, and he never pressures me," I looked at Madison, who gave me the side eye, "I was nervous as hell when I first told him, though," I giggled.

"How'd he react to that news?" She leaned in closer, anxious to know more.

I smiled and started blushing, "He told me he'd wait since he is going to be my husband. I thought that was so sweet," I grinned from ear to ear.

Madison cupped her mouth, "Girl, ya'll so mushy. That's sweet, though; you know I'm a hopeless romantic," Madison turned her gaze to the road, "But for real, y'all ain't doing nothing? Just kissing?" She eyed me from the side again.

I looked in the rearview mirror for a moment, "Well…we have tried oral sex."

She waved her hands, "What? Wait, so you sucked his dick?" Madison shouted and faced me, resting her elbow on the console.

"Uh, no, what do I look like?" I wrinkled my brows.

"Well, you said WE, which means you are an equal participant. You could have just said he ate your coochie." She laughed and held her stomach, "You had me shocked for a second," Madison relaxed into her seat, "Well, spill it…was it good?"

I smacked my lips, "Girl, it was," I wiggled in my seat, thinking about how good his tongue felt sucking on my clit. I shook my head to get the thoughts out, "He got that magic tongue."

Madison placed her hand over her mouth and laughed, "Look at you, oooh wee! I'm jealous," she sucked air in between her teeth, "I need to get me some; it's been too damn long, you hear me?" Then, she leaned towards me and stared me dead in the eyes to emphasize the length of time.

I tapped her hand, "Tell me what happened with you and Jhace?"

She paused, as tears rolled down her cheek, "Where do I start?" She released an exasperated sigh, "His ass cheated," she wiped the tears from her face.

My voice inflected, "How did you find out?" my eyes lowered.

"My goofy ass popped up on him on Valentine's Day," she inhaled slowly, "I took the bus to surprise him. I suppose he thought I was the delivery guy or something; his dumb ass swung the door open without checking and stood there with his mouth covered, wearing boxers, and the chick who was in there yelled out, 'Who is dat bitch' when she saw me slap him," she sobbed harder.

I lifted both eyebrows in disbelief, "I am so sorry. I hadn't even realized it's been that long since the breakup."

"Because you been M.I.A. Why do you think I was blowing up your phone that night? I needed someone to talk to, but you were too busy to answer the phone," Madison crossed her arms and cut her eyes in my direction.

I gently squeezed her hand, "I'm sorry, girl, had I known, I would have answered the phone." It hit me hard that I wasn't a good friend these past few months because I had been self-absorbed in my world, "I promise to be a better friend," I rubbed her back.

When we made it to the Isle, the traffic was bumper to bumper, and the music was blasting. Women wore their booty shorts and tight shirts, showing off everything, and the men were shirtless. We parked, got out, and leaned against the door to peep the scene. In no more than five minutes, two dusty-ass dudes approached us. One had on a durag and a dingy wife beater. The other guy looked just as bad, his teeth were yellow, and it looked like a tooth was missing from the side. Madison didn't care if either of the guys heard her; she leaned over, "Girl, what the hell? I know they are not coming over here," she swayed her head left and right and extended her arm. She was so loud she caught the attention of a group of dudes who stood in front of a Denali parked across from us.

"Say, y'all out here looking fine as hell. Can we chill over here with y'all?" The one who wore the dingy wife beater asked.

"Naw, me and my girl, we good," Madison reached over and placed her arm around my waist, pulling me closer to her.

"Yo girl," the other guy spoke and grabbed the bulge in the front of his dark jeans, "What that 'posed to mean?"

"As in my girl, my bitch, my Lady," Madison leaned her head to the side.

"Stop playing; y'all not together," they said in unison.

Without warning, Madison placed her index finger under my chin, turned my head, and pressed her lips against mine. Instinctively, I moved my lips with hers, and she parted mine, sliding her tongue into my mouth. In shock, I moved back and wiped my mouth.

"Well, forget y'all," they waved their hands and walked away. I waited until they were out of sight before pinching Madison on the arm, "Why the hell did you do that?"

"Chill girl, those dudes were not going to leave us alone," she placed her hands on her hip, "I only kissed you as a repellent, and it worked." She reached into the car to grab her lip gloss from her bag. She rubbed her arm, "That shit hurt you pinch like an old lady."

"That was foul. What am I going to tell Christian?" I walked over to her and stood behind her. Madison bent over to look at her reflection in the passenger side mirror.

She faced me, "Nothing; why would you tell him anything?" She pressed her lips together and raised her brow, "It was a joke — we got them from over here, didn't we? So, stop tripping," she said, annoyed.

I walked away and got into the 'Vette slamming the door. I overheard the people in the truck next to us whisper, "Ohh, girl, she big mad," frustrated I turned up the radio and reached into the glove department to throw on my shades. Madison rolled her eyes and walked across the street to the Denali. She approached a group of young men wearing gold boots, camo pants, and purple tops. George Clinton's *Atomic Dog* played loudly, and they jumped around with their tongues hanging out, swinging their arms, barking. A crowd of girls gathered and bobbed their heads to the music.

I hopped out of my car and sat on the hood to watch. There was no cloud in sight, and I pressed the back of my hand against my forehead to wipe the sweat. Then, I noticed one of the guys open up a cooler and reach inside. He nodded his head in my direction and held up a can. I turned, looking to my left and right to check if he may have been signaling one of his friends. "I'm talking to you," he yelled before he walked over, "I know you hot over here sitting on the hood of your car. You like grape pop?" he handed me the can of Faygo.

"Thanks," I opened the can and took a gulp, "Whew, this is so good."

"You're welcome; I'm Miles," he extended his hand and waited for me to introduce myself.

"I'm Essence," I squinted my eyes and looked across the street at Madison.

"Your girl kind of wild," Miles leaned against my car, "Are y'all together for real?"

I shook my head, "Uh no, she's my best friend," I looked at the ground, embarrassed he saw the kiss.

He wiped his forehead, "The kiss looked pretty serious," he chuckled, "I noticed you around Morrall; you run track, right?" he squinted.

"Yup, you go there too?" I saw his Cadmus Cougar lanyard hanging from his pocket.

"Yeah, it's my sophomore year. What year are you in?" Miles sipped his pop.

"I just started my sophomore year, too," I smiled.

"That's what's up," he tossed his can in the trash, "I never see you at any of the parties. So, you must don't get out?" Miles smiled.

"I do; I don't go to parties though. Usually, I'm with my boyfriend," I pulled my sunglasses back down over my eyes.

"Oh, so you aren't single," he stepped back and grinned, "And why are you covering up those pretty eyes?" Miles pulled my sunglasses off and sat them on the car's hood, "That's better;

my parents taught me it was always polite to make eye contact when you're talking to someone."

I raised my brow, surprised at his assertiveness, "Okay," I chuckled, "Is this better?" I asked playfully, opening my eyes wider.

"Much better. So, is your man Greek?" He leaned against the car again.

"No, he's not Greek. He used to play basketball for Morrall; you may know him," I remember the championship picture in his apartment.

"Naw, I don't know many athletes," Miles interjected, "I got Economics 101 with you."

I narrowed my eyes, "I thought you looked familiar," I smiled, nudging him on the arm.

Miles grinned, "I'm surprised you didn't recognize me before from staring at you, but then again, you barely look away from your notes," he laughed harder. "If I'm not overstepping, maybe we can exchange numbers and study sometimes — if that's okay."

I hummed, "Give me your number; when we have the next exam, I'll reach out," I handed him my cell phone.

Miles saved his number, "It was nice chatting with you. Let me get back to my frat brothers; talk to you soon," Miles jogged across the street.

The crowd lightened up a bit, but Madison was still lit. She was bent over, hands on her knees, shaking her ass on a dude who danced behind her. I shook my head; she always was the life of the party and never knew a stranger. Unfortunately, people assumed she overdid everything because of how she looked. She was known for being fast, and boys often used her for money and anything you could get out of her. Puberty did her the worst, she tried every facial product sold on the market, but her acne never let up. Overnight, Madison went from a shy preteen to an overly sexual teenager open to experimenting. Despite her skin, I thought she was pretty. She was 5'0", yellow bone, rocked a pixie cut, and had Hennessy brown eyes. Unfortunately, her weight fluctuated between 150 to 180 pounds from going through a period of yo-yo dieting. I loved our friendship but felt the strain, and the longer I watched Madison gyrate, her carefree attitude showed me how further we were growing apart.

The sky turned a burnt orange; Madison eventually staggered across the street. She stumbled, and I jumped off the hood to help her into the car, "You okay, girl?" She slurred and cut her eyes at me, "Don't tell me you're still mad about that kiss?" She reached over and laid her hand on my lap.

I rolled my eyes and moved her hand, "Uh, no, but I am irritated that you're drunk," I looked at her, "We don't hang out that much, and instead of catching up, you spent your time getting drunk and acting like a ho," I sighed and shook my head, "But if you had fun, I had fun too," I lifted one brow.

Madison sucked her teeth, "I guess," she turned her head and rested it against the passenger side window.

We rode in silence for the rest of the ride home. Finally, I approached Madison's house and secretly thanked God the evening was over, and I could see Christian soon. I parked the car, "It was nice hanging out with you," I glanced out the window.

"My bad about earlier. I hope you keep it to yourself and not be so inclined to tell your man." She unbuckled her seatbelt, "Besides, if you tell Christian we kissed, you might as well tell him about Miles." Madison cracked the car door and side-eyed me.

I pressed my lips together, "What's there to tell? It was just a joke, right?" I grabbed her hand.

Madison pulled her arm and giggled, "Right. Everything ain't meant to be shared," she pursed her lips, "I may not be a relationship guru, but I know some things are for yourself," she hurried out of her seat and slammed the door.

I rolled the window down, "So, you won't say anything either, right?" I leaned over and looked at her.

"Secret safe with me. Good night," Madison gave me the deuces and closed her front door.

I shook my head; what did I get myself into? Christian and I were transparent with each other. *The kiss was innocent,* I thought, but I couldn't help but think back to it; her kiss was alluring. I felt guilty and slightly dirty knowing I made out with my best friend and secretly enjoyed it. I bit my bottom lip and nodded. *Get yourself together*, I thought. Tomorrow, I have dinner plans with my parents and Christian; the last thing I needed was a distraction.

Chapter Six

CHRISTIAN

I reserved a table at a high-scale restaurant on the top floor of the Detroit Riverside Casino. The view was perfect; you could see the city and the Canadian bridge. The host escorted me to the table, and I patiently waited for Essence and her parents to arrive. The four-star menu was impressive, and I dressed formally for the occasion, wearing a tailored suit, burgundy suede jacket, and black slacks. Essence smiled hard as she walked in with her parents; she was breathtaking. She wore a black fitted dress that showed considerable cleavage but was still tasteful. Her multicolored statement necklace was an excellent choice; very elegant. Her father wore a gray suit, and her mother wore a silver gown; her parents often matched out in public. I leaned down, and Essence threw her arms around my neck. "You smell good," she kissed my ear, instantly turning me on.

"Thank you, baby," I slid a chair out from beneath the table, "You look magnificent as always." I walked over to her mother, kissed her cheek, and shook Mr. Donaldson's hand. "I'm glad you can join Essence and me for dinner."

"What's the special occasion?" Essence eyed the chandeliers throughout the restaurant.

"I'm glad you asked," I said as I looked over to Mr. Donaldson, giving him the queue.

He cleared his throat, "The firm likes the job Christian has been doing, and we have decided to hire him full term," Mr. Donaldson gripped my hand.

Essence gasped; she leaned over and pressed her lips against mine, "I am so proud of you," she looked into my eyes and leaned back in her chair.

The waiter returned with a tray of champagne, a pecan-crusted red snapper for Mrs. Donaldson, lobster bisque for Essence, Chef's chicken for me, and a ribeye for Mr. Donaldson. We finished dinner, and the waiter served crème brulee for dessert. Essence looked around the table, "So they forgot all about my dessert?" she chuckled.

"Baby, just chill; yours is coming," I pointed at the server who carried the silver-domed, gourmet tray with her dessert.

"Talk about the presentation, all of this for a molted chocolate cake?" She smiled and danced in her seat.

The waiter lifted the lid, and on the plate revealed the words, 'Will you marry me?' drizzled in chocolate sauce surrounding a red box; I got on one knee and held her hand, "Essence, you're all my heart wants. You make loving me look easy. God out did Himself when he created you; He knew exactly what I needed," I opened the red Cartier box, displayed the 2.5-carat princess cut diamond, and placed the ring on her finger, "Would you do me the honor of marrying me?"

Essence fanned her face; tears dripped out the corner of her eyes. Finally, she nodded and stood up, "Yes," she threw her arms around me.

Her mom smiled widely, "Let me see it, baby," she held her hand, gazing at the ring she helped pick out. A few weeks back, I asked the Donaldsons' permission to marry Essence. Mrs. Donaldson held Essence's hand, admiring the diamond. "It looks perfect! Congratulations on your engagement," she kissed Essence's cheek and walked over and hugged me, "I'm so glad you'll officially be a part of the family, my bonus son," she grinned.

Mr. Donaldson asked for the check. "I think it's about time to let you two love birds celebrate the rest of the evening. Congratulations again," he stood up from the table, extended his hand, and pulled me closer, wrapping his arm around my neck, "You be sure to make my daughter happy," he whispered into my ear.

We left the restaurant and went to my Redford home, which I inherited when my mom died. I planned the evening weeks ago and got Ava's buy-in; she even offered to plan a romantic evening for Essence and me indoors. While heading home, I texted Ava to make sure she completed everything. We parked, and

Essence and I saw the candlelight flickering through the window; I opened the front door; red and white tea lit candles lit a pathway from the dining, living room, and bedroom. Musiq Soulchild's *Aimewitue* played softly. Essence threw her head back, "You're full of surprises, I see," she placed her head on my arm, "This is so lovely!" She looked around the room, not breaking her gaze.

I grabbed her hand and pulled her into my body; we swayed slowly to the music as I sang the lyrics of the song into her ear, "You are the most beautiful woman I've laid eyes on, and from this day forward, I will do anything to keep this look on your face," I whispered in Essence's ears. Our fingers interlocked, and I led her to the bedroom, "Get undressed; I have another surprise for you," I handed her a plush white bathrobe and slippers, then closed the door behind me.

Essence giggled, "Christian, you're going to spoil me if you keep doing this," She twisted the knob and stepped out into the hallway biting her bottom lip and sucking gently. Essence grabbed my belt buckle and pulled me closer, "I'm ready for my surprise," she stood on her tiptoes, puckering her lips. We kissed deeply, and she pulled my shirt out of my pants and unbuttoned it slowly. Her hands glided across my shoulder, and my shirt fell to the floor. Essence continued to caress my skin; her fingertips caressed underneath my chest, "What's this, Christian?" She stepped back and narrowed her eyes to get a closer look.

"It's nothing, baby," I grabbed my shirt and slid my arm into the sleeve, "It's a scar from my incision," I looked down, embarrassed she noticed it. I worked extra hard in the gym, building my pectoral muscles to hide the scarring. Essence noticed the change in my demeanor,

"You don't have to put your shirt on, baby," she grabbed my arm, "What kind of surgery did you have?"

I exhaled and looked down, "I was in a horrible accident years ago that caused one of my lungs to collapse and some other complications."

Essence wrapped her arm around herself, "I'm sorry. Is that why you stopped playing ball?"

There were many things I should have told Essence before I proposed. But, until now, we were both honest with each other, or I planned to be—for the most part, "Yup, that's one of the reasons," I opened the door to the bathroom, wanting to divert her attention, "Tonight, let's talk about our future, and leave the past alone for now."

The flames from the candles illuminated the bathroom; Ava filled the tub with rose peddles and bubbles; Essence beamed, "This is gorgeous," she stepped out of her slippers and untied her bathrobe, and I watched it hit the ground. I bent down, placed my arm beneath her legs, lifted her from the floor, and placed her into the bathtub gently. Lavender filled our noses; I stood back up and slid my shirt off, hanging it on the knob. I kneeled in front of the tub and draped my arms into the water to feel the warmth.

"This water feels so good, baby, thank you," Essence looked me in the eyes, "You not planning on joining me, are you?" She smiled.

Nodding my head, I leaned over, grabbed a washcloth, and soaked it. I let the water trickle down her back and listened to her moan as she tilted her head back and closed her eyes, "Tonight is all about me pleasing and pampering you, my love," I kissed her forehead.

After her bath, I dried her body and carried her into a different room with a massage table. I poured her a glass of non-alcoholic wine and handed her the wineglass. "Sip slow," I joked. Essence turned her glass up and consumed all the contents. I took her glass, directed her to lie on her stomach, then grabbed the massage oil and poured it into my large hands. I tilted my hand and watched the oil drip across her spine and run down her back. I made long, smooth, circular strokes, kneading her muscles with my fingers. "Turn over," she laid on her back, and her nipples hardened; I poured oil on her breasts, and she flinched and nibbled her lip. My hands gently glided across her breasts and massaged the oil into her skin. She exhaled slowly, and her chest rose and fell as I rubbed my thumbs across her nipples and squeezed.

I spread her legs and listened to her moans as I poured oil on her vagina, and watched it drip down to her clitoris. I massaged her bikini line gradually, sliding my palms over her pussy, teasing her with my fingertips. Finally, I slid my middle finger in and out of her opening. Her walls contracted, and my finger glistened with her warm nectar. I pulled her closer and placed the tip of my tongue on her clitoris, licking up and down.

Essence grabbed the back of my head, held me in place, and whispered, "Oh yes, you feel so good, baby." I put my mouth on her vagina, sliding my tongue in and out of her opening. She pumped my face. I watched her grip her nipples and rest her palms on her breasts. Her clit was enlarged, making it easy to suck. She throbbed in my mouth as I licked her faster in circles, "Please let me feel you," she begged, pushing my head deeper into her vagina. I unbuttoned my pants, letting them fall to the floor, climbed on the massage table, and pressed my lips against her mouth. Essence wrapped her legs around my waist, and I could feel her hands slide into my briefs as she grabbed my ass, "Take these off; let me feel you inside of me," she insisted.

I took both her hands into mine and held them over her head, "No, not until we are married; just enjoy this," I whispered into her ear and rubbed my body against hers. Her eyes rolled back. We rocked back and forth, and the table squealed. Essence placed her teeth around my bottom lip and sucked it gently into her mouth as I thrust my hips up and down, back and forth, against her pussy. She dug her nails into my skin, "Damn, you feel good, baby," I whispered and placed my hand underneath her head, "Cum for me, baby." Essence squealed; I looked into her eyes. A stream of water flowed from the corner of her right eye. I placed my thumb on her cheek and wiped it away, "I love you, baby."

"Promise you'll love me like this forever," Essence said.

I sensed the seriousness in the tone of her voice. I looked deep into her eyes, and without hesitation, I replied, "Forever and always."

Chapter Seven

ESSENCE

Christian and I planned to have a spring wedding, which gave us less than a year to plan perfectly. My dad wasn't feeling the idea of us living together unwed, and as much as I hated living apart, I knew it was best since I craved more of him since the proposal; I'd already come close to having sex with him.

My parents were having their annual New Year's Eve party, and I hoped to see Madison there. We hadn't seen much of each other and hardly spoke since hanging out on the Isle. With track practice, classes, and meeting with wedding planners, I barely had time for myself. However, we had to catch up, and I wanted to ask her, officially, to be my maid of honor. When we were younger, we agreed to be at each other's weddings, and despite the distance, it meant a lot for her to be in mine still.

It looked like a winter wonderland when I arrived at my parent's. My dad covered the house with so many Christmas lights; it lit up half the block. My mother had a thing for Christmas trees. Every room had a fully decorated tree; she draped garland around the stairwell, wreaths hung on the walls, and stockings dangled over the fireplace. She always went overboard with holiday decorations, switching out the living room furniture and replacing it with white leather furniture because she wanted to make her red and green snowflake throw pillows pop.

While Christian mingled with the partners from the firm, I helped my mother prepare the food. Then, I felt my cell phone vibrate; I reached into my pocket and saw Madison calling. Unfortunately, she ran exceptionally late and called two hours earlier, claiming to be on her way. I sighed, "Hey, what's up? Where are you?"

"Sorry, Essence, I'm on my way—I was running behind. Is it cool if I brought a guest?" She giggled.

"Yeah, that's cool. I can't talk though, so get here," I hang up, irritated Madison would be no help like she usually was. Another hour had passed, and there was still no sign of her. Everyone finished their first round of food and was working on seconds. Christian and I spent time working the room as I introduced him to my family, who were excited to hear about our engagement.

I eyed my phone, "Is everything alright?" Christian rubbed my shoulders to calm me. It was nearing eleven o'clock, and Madison was still not there.

"Yeah, I'm good, just wondering where Madison is," I exhaled, disappointed in her no-show, "I'm about to grab some more eggnog. Did you need anything?" Halfway into the kitchen, I heard the doorbell ring. I answered the door and smiled, quickly forgetting how angry I was at her. Madison being here was all that mattered now.

"Sorry it took me so long," she tapped the shoulder of her guest, signaling him to turn around, "I picked up Miles; he didn't have New Year's plan," she smiled.

My smile instantly faded. *Typical Madison bullshit,* I thought, "Really?" I squinted my eyes and gave a half smile.

Madison raised her brow. Reading my expression, she said, "You said it was cool to bring a guest. If I knew it was going to be a big deal, I wouldn't have come," she stepped inside the house.

I waved my hand, dismissing her comment. "She can show you where to hang your coat," I looked at Miles, who stood frozen with his hand over his mouth, unsure how to react.

Miles cleared his throat. "Um, I didn't know it was your party I was coming to."

I folded my arms across my chest, "I'm sure, but you're here now, so don't worry about it," I pointed towards the dining area, "The food's in there—help yourself to anything you like."

I waited until he was out of sight before I pulled Madison into the guest bathroom, "What is up with you? First, you come late to the party, then bring Miles; you know you should have told me he was coming," I yelled, clenching my teeth.

Madison narrowed her eyes, "I honestly didn't think you would mind. I ran into Miles a few weeks back on campus, and we just started hanging out. From what he told me, you two never spoke since seeing each other." Madison reached for my hand, "You're engaged?" Her voice lightened, and her eyes focused on my ring. She pursed her lips, "I guess Mile's up for grabs."

I scoffed and rolled my eyes, "It's not about that, Madison; just forget it," I stared at her, and tears filled my eyes. "We barely hang out, and when we do, I don't know," unsure what words to choose. "I just wanted to hang with you, catch up, and at least ask you to be my maid of honor," I ran my hands through my hair and forced a smile.

Madison leaned her back against the door. "Surprised you asked me to be in the wedding," she crossed her arms, "Don't you think it's a little too soon to marry him, though? Y'all barely know each other," she lowered her eyes eying the ring again.

I pressed my lips together and looked her up and down, "Wow," I shook my head, "Why can't you be happy for me? Lately, I don't know what's been going on with you. Are you jealous that you don't have a man?" I placed my hands on my waist.

Madison threw her hands up, "Look. I didn't mean anything by it. I support whatever you choose to do, but as your friend, I had to ask." She darted her eyes toward the floor. We were silent for a few minutes, "I think I should go," she walked out of the bathroom, grabbed her and Miles's coats from the closet, "Let's dip," he was finishing up his plate of food.

Miles narrowed his brows, "Already?"

Christian, unsure of what was happening, walked into the hallway, "You finally made it?" He hugged Madison.

"Yes, but we are heading out," Madison let go of his embrace, turned around, and headed out the door with Miles.

I sat down on the staircase and placed my hand over my face trying to conceal the tears streaming from my eyes. Christian sat next to me and rubbed my back; we sat silently for a few minutes, "I don't know what's going on with Madison," my lips quivered as I sobbed.

Christian wiped my tears. "I don't want to be out of place, saying this since Madison's your girl, but I think she may be jealous of you," he shook his head, pressing his lips.

I shrugged, "Maybe, so," I wiped my face and exhaled, "We kissed," I covered my mouth as soon as the words slipped from my lips, shocked that I'd told him.

Christian eyes widened, "Today?" His eyebrows creased, and he raised his brow.

I turned my head, "No, the night we hung out at the Isle," I paused before looking him in the eyes, "I'm sorry I didn't tell you before—it wasn't like how it sounds. Two guys tried to talk to us, so we acted like we were together, and she kissed me. I was shocked when it happened," I buried my face into my hands. I could hear Christian laugh, which gave me a sense of relief. He winked, "Yeah, she is jealous; she likes you," he chuckled.

Thinking back to that day, I cringed. The kiss hadn't crossed my mind in a while, but what else could it be? Her behavior was unexplainable. She was like a ticking bomb, and I didn't know what to expect from her. It was outlandish, Madison showing up with Miles, and although I hadn't called him, she knew what she was doing; I felt like she was taking a dig at me. I sat on the stairs with a blank stare.

Christian broke the silence, "My baby kissing girls now?" He nudged me. "I'm not mad at you; you're irresistible," he held my hand gently, "Just give her some time—she won't stay mad," he stood up and grabbed my hands; he looked down at his watch it was minutes away from midnight, "Let's go find us a mistletoe."

I followed him into the living room. He pulled me under the doorway and wrapped his arms around me. Everyone in the room picked up their wine glasses and gathered around the 70" flat screen; my mom set the channel to see the ball drop. We all watched and counted counterclockwise. Then, in unison, the guests shouted, "Happy New Year." Christian held me tight and gave me the most sensual kiss I'd ever felt. Maybe marrying Christian was too soon. But everything felt right, right, or wrong; I couldn't wait to be Mrs. Powell.

Chapter Eight

CHRISTIAN

My eyes bolted open, and I sat up in the middle of the bed, my heart pounding against my chest. My sweat soaked the sheets, and I scanned the pitch-black room and quickly found the red lights on the alarm clock that read 3:43 AM. I hadn't gotten a whole night's rest, the past few weeks, I had awakened to the same nightmare. I got out of bed and walked into the bathroom, turned on the cold water, cupped my hands, splashed the cool water against my face, and then looked at my reflection in the mirror. *I'm fucked!* I thought.

My wedding was right around the corner, Essence and I planned the most luxurious wedding for months. The guest list primarily consisted of her family and a mixture of our friends. When I met Essence, I told her I was adopted, which is true, but when she asked if I had other relatives, I lied. I hated lying to

Essence, especially since she's been so honest with me, but it was hard to admit the only known family I had—my twin—was not in my life. I didn't want to explain the who, what, and where and I refused to go into the why. It was easier to say I had no family. I hadn't seen or heard from Kristofer for years after he enlisted in the army, and my hatred towards him grew when he failed to show up at mom's funeral.

On numerous occasions, I wanted to tell Essence my secret, but when I opened my mouth, the sharp pain in my stomach was my body's fight-or-flight response. I knew if I told Essence the truth, she would leave, or worse; she'd hate me forever. I wiped the sweat from my brow and clenched my jaw. Then, everything went dark; I didn't realize I had fainted until I heard Essence scream my name. I blinked slowly, opening the slits of my eyes, and saw her leaning over me, trembling with her hands over her mouth. "Are you okay?" Essence helped me up. "Should I call 9-1-1?" She held the phone in her hand.

I got up from the floor, "I'm alright, don't call," Essence looked troubled; I assured her I was okay and just needed sleep. I closed my eyes tight and shook my head, trying to get the thought of my secret being exposed out my head. Finally, I entered the room to lie down, only having a few hours of sleep, which I desperately needed. Mr. Donaldson had been mentoring me, and I was due in the courtroom in the afternoon.

I walked past the soundproof, premier suite, holding my head down; I showed up 30 minutes late and was in no shape to perform in court. My guilt was distracting; it showed I was tardy several times a week and had poorly organized files. Although I attended meetings, my thoughts were scattered. Eventually, one of the partners called me out for staring at a blank legal pad during the staff meeting without taking any notes. Following the meeting, Essence's father met to discuss my decreased performance. Mr. Donaldson cut me some slack; I convinced him I was experiencing wedding jitters. Call it nepotism; one of the other partners would have terminated me if they had seen my performance plummeting.

Mr. Donaldson allowed me to leave early for the day. As I drove home, I heard the muffled sound from my cellular phone that rang inside my briefcase. I answered, "Hey baby, how was court?" Essence had excitement in her voice.

I sighed, "I didn't make it."

"Aww babe, I'm sorry," she paused, "Will you be coming back to campus?"

I exhaled slowly, "I'm kind of tired, babe, I have an early meeting, so I'm staying in the city," I lied. Then, following my fainting episode and Essence finding me passed out, I used the excuse of disappointing her father; God forbid he found out we had been living under the same roof.

"Humph, you sure everything okay?" She exhaled. I could tell she was disappointed.

"Everything's fine, babe. I'll see you soon. I love you," I ended the call. I couldn't bear hearing the sadness in her voice. My secrets weighed on me like a ton of bricks, and I was terrified everything would come crashing down. I arrived home, immediately took my suit jacket off, and loosened my tie heading over to the bar to pour a double shot of Hennessey. I gulped the alcohol, turned on the stereo surround sound, and played *I Love You More Than You'll Ever Know* by Donny Hathaway. I poured another shot of Hennessy and slumped down on the couch, this time sipping the liquor. My eyes felt heavy, and I shut them briefly but was interrupted by a noise coming from the back door. I walked over to the blinds and narrowed my eyes to get a better view but seen nothing. I sat back on the couch and was startled again by the sound of the knob twisting. I walked to the closet, grabbed the steel bat, and gripped it tightly. Thinking *could it be another intruder?*

I looked out the peephole but saw no one; my breath quickened as I turned the locks and cracked the door. I peered my head out and walked out on the porch, ready to knock the hell out of the first person I saw. Instead, a loud thud came from inside my house. I sprinted inside; my heart thumped. The noise was coming from the bathroom. My hands shook as I gripped the bat tighter, "I have a gun," I yelled, hoping it would scare away the intruder; instead, the door flew open. I used all my force and swung the bat as hard as possible but missed and struck the wall missing the stranger as he ducked.

"Aye yo, it's me," the voice sent chills up my spine; it was familiar. I stood frozen and heard the loud clink of the bat as I dropped it. I flicked the lights on, "It's just me," my twin brother Kristofer said with his palms in the air.

"Kristofer!" I shouted, unable to move. I stood fixed and gazed with my mouth open. He stepped closer and threw his arms around me, "What are you doing here?" I stepped away from his embrace.

He grinned, "The army discharged me, so I'm home for good." Kristofer stepped back and eyed me up and down. His brows raised, "Wow, Christian, I didn't know what to expect; you look so different," he placed his hand over his mouth.

I put the bat against the wall, "It's been years—people evolve," I crossed my arms, realizing those bricks were starting to come crashing down on me.

"I know, but I just didn't expect you to look like," he paused to gather his thoughts, "You look like me," Kristofer circled me, "C'mon last, I had seen you, you were beginning your transition journey, you still looked like my sister, but now," he placed his hand beneath his chin, "I'm impressed."

I scoffed and lowered my eyes, "Why are you here? I would think this was the last place you'd show up to since you decided not to come to your mother's funeral," I walked over to the couch and placed my hands in my pocket.

Kristofer let out an exasperated sigh, "I owe you an apology. We weren't on the best terms when I left." He sat next to me and looked me in the eye, "It made matters worse when I didn't show up to the funeral, but on my last tour, I did a lot of thinking about why I enlisted," he sighed and continued. "I was angry; I felt like I was losing my sister; you and mom didn't seem to understand. Mom always favored you growing up, and I was reminded of that when she told me to 'Think of my brother's feelings' as though I didn't have a sister, and I had to let go of her," he blinked tears and looked down toward the ground.

We sat in silence. I thought about what Kristofer shared, and for the first time, I understood. I never imagined how he felt about me transitioning, "You want something to drink?" I pointed at the bar; I walked over and grabbed another glass to pour him a shot of Henny and watched him empty it.

"For whatever it's worth, I'm here now, and hopefully, we can mend things; we all we got." Kristofer and I drank the entire bottle and opened a new one, and I sat listening to him tell me about the tours he'd done while he was in the army. He had traveled and seen the world; he beamed as he told me his war stories. It felt good seeing my brother again, "Enough about me, tell me what's been up with you," he slurred.

I pinched my nose, "Me, wow, you missed a lot! Where do I start?" I slurred, "I'm getting married in two months," I took another sip of Hennessy. "My fiancé's name is Essence."

Kristofer cupped his mouth and leaned forward, "That's awesome! This deserves another toast," he patted me on the back and poured two more shots of cognac, "To love and happiness," we tapped our shot glasses. "What's wrong, Christian? It's a celebration," he sat on the couch and pried my hands from my face.

I covered my mouth and mumbled, "She doesn't know," burying my face in my hands.

He furrowed his brows, "Know what?" he sat down, mouth gaped open, "You didn't tell her you got a twin?" he looked even more confused.

I cut him off, "She doesn't know I'm transgender," I rubbed the nape of my neck. I got up from the couch and paced the floor, "I'm petrified of telling her the truth. You didn't want anything to do with mom or me because I was transgender, and she accepted it," I slumped my shoulders. Tears trickled down my face, "You don't know what it's like knowing you're a man but stuck in the wrong body," I wiped away my tears, "I contemplated suicide once and even wished I were you sometimes; I was so uncomfortable in this body."

I remember hating to wear dresses; I felt my masculinity was insulted. So, when I started dressing like a guy, it felt normal. For years I pretended to be a tomboy to get away with wearing your clothes until mom sat me down; we had a long talk. Ultimately, I was honest about not being a lesbian and explained I felt like I was a boy.

Kristofer stared at me with wide eyes, "That's deep, Christian. I should have been a better brother towards you; I'm your twin." We made eye contact, "But you have to tell Essence — I know you're scared, but you can't continue to hide who you are," he placed his hand on my back, "You aren't allowing her to love the real you; that's unfair to you and her. I don't even know how you managed to get away with it so far," he shook his head.

I shrugged my shoulder, "Honestly, it's not hard as it seems; she's a virgin," I said.

"That can only work for so long, though, because she's gone expect to consummate the marriage," Kristofer took another sip of liquor.

I hunched my shoulders and looked down at the ground taking long blinks. I was quiet for minutes. "Maybe not," there was a sudden change in my demeanor, "What if you were me, just until I recover from surgery?" I stood up and paced the floor. "My surgery is in six months, and then there's recovery. So, you would only need to sleep with Essence for a little while," I made eye contact with Kristofer, whose eyes were even bigger this time.

"Hell no!" He stood up from the couch, walked to the other side of the room, and glared at me, "You're drunk—and desperate," he shook his head, "This is beyond crazy. Do you even hear yourself right now?" Kristofer narrowed his eyes.

"Man, please," I got off the couch, kneeling in front of him, tears streaming down my face, "I can't lose her; I'll do anything, and I'll pay you," I pleaded. "You owe me for abandoning mom and me," I got off the floor and stood in front of him, crossing my arms.

He clenched his jaws and shook his head, "All right, all right, all right—I'll help you," he yelled, "Let me be clear, I don't agree with it, but I need the money," he placed his palm on his forehead and exhaled slowly, "Maybe if I were supportive and around, you wouldn't be in this mess." Kristofer sat back down and sipped his Hennessy. "How much money are you talking about anyway?" His demeanor perked up.

I looked at the ceiling, filled my cheek with air, and released an exasperated breath, "How much do you want?"

Kristofer rubbed his chin, "Thirty thousand dollars," he gulped the liquor and slammed the glass on the table.

Then, without hesitation, I extended my hand and said, "Deal." I threw my arms around his neck, embracing him, "I can have your money tomorrow. You saved my life, bro," I smiled.

We devised a plan for the remainder of the night, and if executed correctly, I would have everything I wanted: to marry the woman of my dreams and have bottom surgery, all without blowing my cover. I told Kristofer about Essence and how I'd fallen in love with her. The weight eased off my chest, and I felt a sense of relief for the first time in months. The next day I withdrew the $30K from the bank and then dropped my brother off at a hotel. We decided it would be best for him to stay far away from the Redford home to prevent our cover from being blown.

Traffic was moderately low Saturday morning. I hit the 96-West freeway and drove back to campus. It was just past 10:00 AM, and the sky was bright and sunny without a cloud. I stopped by a local florist, picked up some lily flowers, and headed to Essence's apartment she got her sophomore year. The apartment was quiet as I entered. I placed my briefcase on the dining room table and walked to her room. I sat down on the edge of the bed and watched Essence, who lay peacefully. *Her face is perfect,* I thought as I softly leaned over her and pressed my lips against hers. Her breasts rose and fell beneath the sheets; I undressed, leaving on my briefs.

I entered the bathroom and quickly closed the door behind me; locking the bathroom door became second nature to me, always being careful not to get caught. The bathroom filled with steam; I pulled my briefs down and took off the silicone packer I wore daily to give the illusion of a natural penis. It was so realistic I could stand to pee, and it matched my skin tone. I stared at my reflection, admiring my muscular frame, but I was disappointed when I looked down at my vagina; I was dissatisfied. Gender dysphoria was real; constantly seeing my vagina reminded me I had the wrong body. I was anxious to get approved for bottom surgery so I could finally be the man I was supposed to be. I wiped the steam from the mirror. I admired my arms longer as I stood fixed, gazing at my reflection; I worked hard to get the perfectly sculpted triceps. Then, my eyes continued to wander down to my abdomen. I ran my fingers across my 12-pack, then beneath my chest that hid the scarring from my top surgery, which I had a year and a half ago.

I bathed and then exited the bathroom, Essence was still asleep, and as much as I wanted her to sleep, I craved her. My mouth watered, and I licked my lips. I lifted the comforter and crawled towards her from the foot of the bed. *This woman sleeps like a log;* I thought. She stayed asleep while I slid my hands up her legs and opened them softly. I stuck the tip of my tongue out and parted her lips with my tongue, and she let out a soft moan. Essence wiggled her hips slowly, and I gently moved my hands underneath her body and palmed her ass cheeks. I sucked on her clitoris until I felt her body awaken. She thrust her hips back and forth as my tongue slid inside of her vagina. Essence massaged my head with her fingertips; I was aroused, devouring her pussy, and humping the mattress, fluttering the tip of my tongue up and down her clitoris. Finally, I gripped her ass, "Turn over," I demanded and sat her on my face. Essence gasped; her moans grew louder as she rode my tongue.

"I love when you wake me up like this, baby," Essence moaned, "I'm cumming," and screamed, gyrating until she collapsed on the bed. I crawled on top of her, pressing my lips against hers, and tasted her sweetness. She licked and sucked my bottom lip, and in a low whisper, she said, "I love you, baby."

"I love you too, baby," I turned my back and watched her slide from beneath the covers and walk into the bathroom, "What time did you get in, baby?" She yelled from inside.

I clasped my hands behind my head, looking up at the ceiling, "I got in a half hour ago," my thoughts drifted back to my brother and the plan we discussed.

Essence walked into the room wearing her purple lace teddy, "Did you eat?" she ran her fingers through her untamed hair.

I smiled and licked my lips, "Your sweet stuff," I smirked; I sat up in the bed and patted the mattress, "Come back over here."

Essence walked over and straddled my lap, "Babe, we can't lounge around all day, our wedding is around the corner, and I need your full participation," she pouted her lips.

She had a point; aside from writing checks, I had given little time for planning. I squeezed her hips and looked into her eyes, "I promise I'll do better," I raised my palm.

In the subsequent weeks, I did a 180; I was present at each meeting we had with the wedding planner; I visited the bakery, tasted over 20 flavors of cake, and even gave my input on the floral arrangements. Our wedding day finally arrived, and the guests stood patiently waiting for Essence to walk down the aisle of the glass-enclosed wedding venue. I looked around the greenhouse resembling the botanical gardens; I thought *everything looked* terrific. Colorful floral arrangements were everywhere, and the decorators draped the entrance in all-white curtains. The lighting gave a dramatic touch as the violinist played *Nothing Even Matters* by Lauryn Hill and D'Angelo. My eyes were glued at the end of the aisle as I watched Essence enter the greenhouse wearing a laced, trumpet-styled wedding dress. My cheeks felt flushed, and my body tingled as my eyes filled with water. She was so captivating. Mr. Donaldson walked over to me, gave me a firm handshake, and kissed his baby girl on the cheek before handing Essence over to me so the preacher could officiate the wedding.

To death do us part, I smiled; we were officially Mr. & Mrs. Christian Powell; *we did it,* I thought. Things were going as planned. I arranged for Kristofer to fly to Punta Cana, our honeymoon destination, before Essence and I arrived. My mother left me a fortune in her will, so I rented a private Villa off the beach. We were in Paradise; our main bedroom had a California bed with a view of the ocean, an outdoor shower, and a fully equipped kitchen with a butler and chef; I couldn't ask for more.

Kristofer and I needed to be strategic, ensuring we carried out every detail of the plan. I booked a solo spa massage for Essence, which gave me a two-hour window. The chef prepared a candlelight dinner with a few of her seafood favorites, and I had steak with all its dressing. I reserved a villa for Kristofer, far enough for him not to be spotted but close enough to catch transportation to perform our switches. I picked up the prepaid cell and called him to review the ground rules.

"This place is nice," he walked around the villa admiring the layout, "You sure you want to go through with this? It's not too late to back out," he encouraged leaning against the kitchen island with his brow raised.

I pressed my lips together, "Bro, this my only option, now let me go over the rules," I held a finger up as I spoke each rule; no anal, oral, and don't cum in her," I winced.

Kristofer tilted his head, "Wait a minute; I can't give her oral sex? Wouldn't she expect that?" his brow furrowed.

"You can give her oral, but I don't want her performing oral sex on you," I curled my lip, "It's bad enough you're having sex with my wife."

I discussed the remaining details with Kristofer, and we were both ready for the evening. Essence arrived from her massage relaxed and with an appetite. We enjoyed our dinner and had a few glasses of champagne; she wasn't a drinker, and two glasses had her slurring her words, "I'm so ready to make love to you," she flirted across the table. Essence stood up, stumbled, and grabbed the table's edge to catch her balance. She giggled and straddled my lap, pressing her lips against mine and massaging my tongue with hers. My body felt warm; I desired her and desperately wanted to make love to her instead of Kristofer, but I couldn't. My heart raced, and water streamed from the corners of my eyes. She placed her palm on my chest; we made eye contact, "Don't be nervous." She grabbed my hand, leading me into our bedroom. Her assertiveness was sexy and turned me on.

"We have all night. What's the rush?" I wanted to stall a bit longer. I twisted my ring and looked at Essence. She pushed me onto the bed and mounted me, kissing me passionately this time. She took her shirt off, revealing her perky breasts; I grabbed her arms, trying to control the night's tempo. I didn't plan for improvisation. "I—I," I stuttered and cleared my throat, "I bought you something." I reached for the box wrapped with a ribbon, "Open it and see what it is," I handed it to her; her eyes widened as she pulled the ribbon and opened the box. She looked at the black laced satin teddy and placed it against her body, "Go try it on," I pointed into the bathroom.

Here it was, the opportunity to turn back or let Kristofer switch places. Ignoring my conscious, I waved my hand, and he snuck out of the louvered shutter closet where he'd been hiding. The slits were wide enough to let me peep through the openings. I closed the door, kneeled, and looked out the slits, guaranteeing I didn't miss one minute. Essence returned, dressed in lingerie, and I watched my brother undress. He was in excellent shape and muscular like me. His height towered too, but he was two inches shorter, not something she'd realize. Kristofer's eyes were blue with specks of grey and he had two dimples. Although I made sure we had matching haircuts the day before the honeymoon, we looked identical aside from minor differences in appearance. I swallowed hard, then turned away when I noticed Kristofer's hard erection.

"I'm ready," Essence wrapped her arms around his neck and kissed him intensely.

My brother lay on the bed, hands clasped behind his head, penis sticking up in the air; it was huge. I curled my lips, intimidated by its size. I will never be able to pull this off. I trembled; for the first time, I was ready to call off the plan and come out of the closet. *No surgery would be able to give me a penis like that,* I thought. I reached for the knob and twisted it open, but I was frozen in place with my mouth gaped open when I saw Essence mount Kristofer and slide her vagina on his manhood; I was too late.

Chapter Nine

ESSENCE

We made it to Punta Cana International Airport, ready to depart. Christian forgot something in our shuttle, so he suggested I go through security, and he'd catch up after he checked our bags. Wrapped around the queues were a sea of travelers waiting to reach security. I took off my shoes and jewelry and placed my purse inside a crate waiting for security to signal me to walk through the metal detector. I grabbed my items and sat on the bench, waiting for Christian. We spent a week at the resort, and I observed Christian's temperament go from his cheerful, affectionate self to irritable. On our last day, he barely touched me. As I waited, I thought about the cause of his sudden behavior change; he was distracted and slightly cold. Could it be me? I saw Christian had finished putting on his shoes. I reached for his hand, but he quickly snatched it away.

We boarded the Boeing 747 airplane and found our seats. The silence between Christian and I was awkward, and I felt uneasy, "Baby, talk to me — did I do something wrong?" I reached over and squeezed his hands.

Christian turned his head from the window that held his attention and sighed, "No baby, you didn't do anything. I forgot I have a case to prep when I get home; I'm sorry for being a little inattentive." He leaned over and kissed me.

It seemed unbelievable that he was on our honeymoon and thinking of work. I laid my head on his shoulder, not wanting to press the issue, dozed off and before I knew it, we landed in Detroit.

Energized after napping during the five-hour flight, Christian offered more conversation. Growing up with my father, I saw how demanding being an attorney was. While the ink still needs to dry, I hope Christian didn't switch up yet. It was dusk when we pulled up to Christian's Redford home. He unloaded the luggage, rolled it to the door, Christian placed his arm around my waist, and stuck the key in the lock.

"Hold up, baby. It's tradition for a husband to carry his wife over the threshold," he swooped me into his arms and kissed me, "Much better," he joked and placed my feet on the living room floor.

He finished wheeling all the luggage inside, and I looked at the photos. I wish he had family members to witness our union. Our wedding was lovely; while my family and friends loved

Christian as much as I did, I could only help to imagine how he felt not having any family present. I could tell from looking at the photos his mother adored him. I recalled wanting to have siblings, and from the many conversations Christian and I had, he seemed to enjoy the same sentiment. When Christian and I settled as a couple, I wanted to start a family.

Christian wrapped his arms around me, his lips brushing against my earlobe, "I was thinking of buying a new home," he whispered.

I twirled around and smiled, "Oh my God, I'd love that," I embraced him. "When can we start looking?"

"ASAP. Hopefully, we can close on a new home soon, something that is both of ours," he placed his index finger beneath my chin and lifted my head to stare into my eyes.

"Ours, I like the sound of that," I pulled on Christian's belt buckle. "I've been wanting more of you since we left Punta Cana," I bit my bottom lip and unfastened his jeans.

Christian smiled and stepped backward swiftly, fastening his jeans. "Really? Tell me what you liked the most." Coy, he raised his brows.

I pushed him onto the couch, straddled his lap, and kissed his lips after every word, "I can show you better than I can tell you."

Christian's hands gripped my ass. "Come on, baby, tell me," he pleaded.

I rubbed the back of my neck and chuckled, "You act like you weren't there," I exhaled and stared into his eyes. "I liked how passionate you were, the way you felt inside me," I said before I paused and narrowed my eyes. "Are you making me say all this?"

"Yes, go on," he smirked.

I rested my hands on his chest and felt his heart race. Initially, I thought I turned him on as I stoked his ego, but the way he lowered his eyebrows and jutted his chin, I noticed Christian's face grow angry. "Are you alright?" I looked at his crinkled nose. Christian immediately looked away, lifted me from his lap, and sat me on the couch next to him.

He flashed a half smile. "Yes, I just remembered I have something to grab from the office; it completely slipped my mind," he stood up and scratched his head. Christian could see the confusion on my face. "I won't be long," he grabbed his keys.

"Can't it wait? Technically, we're still on our honeymoon, and you don't have to return to work for another week." I stood up and placed my hands on my waist.

"I promise I'll make it quick," he smiled. "While I'm gone, you can look at some properties online and pick out anything you want." He kissed my forehead and headed out the door.

Chapter Ten

CHRISTIAN

I fed the slot machine $100, waiting on my brother Kristofer to arrive from the airport. *I wouldn't say I like gambling, but here I am, gambling my marriage away*, I thought, looking at my watch every minute, hoping he'd arrive. I clenched my jaw the longer I waited, shifting in the swivel chair. Everyone's eyes were glued to me after I slammed my fist on the slot machine. I damn near pulled the lever off. The guy behind me assumed I had lost and handed me a $20 bill from his thousand-dollar jackpot earnings. If only financial losses were my worries.

Gambling was counterproductive, and it didn't take my mind off reality. I sat fixed, staring at the slot machine and going over the worst-case scenario; Kristofer showed up at my Redford home, telling Essence everything. Startled, I jumped from the pat on the shoulder. I turned and clenched my fist, "What took you so fucking long?" I pointed my finger in his face.

Kristofer swatted my hand, "Man, dead all that. They lost my luggage, and it took a while to catch a cab," he said as he sat down at the empty slot machine next to me.

"Don't get comfortable; we have to talk," I got up from the chair to head towards the exit, but Kristofer pulled out a $100 bill, unphased by my demands. I snatched the money, "We need to talk NOW." I looked down at my watch and tapped my foot repeatedly, "I've waited over two hours; I told Essence I wouldn't take long."

Kristofer cracked a half smile. "We can't leave the Mrs. waiting. All night sex-session?" He grinned; his sarcasm annoyed me.

The veins throbbed in my neck, "Would you stop with the damn jokes?" I slammed my fist on the chair.

"Stop being sensitive; I was just playing," he grinned and followed me to the elevator. Eventually, we made it to the suite; Kristofer walked in and fell on his bed. I leaned against the desk. He tapped his fingers against the mattress, "What's so important that you left your wife to come and talk to me?"

I paced back and forth. "We shouldn't continue with the plan. Instead, I'll buy a good strap and do what I gotta do to satisfy Essence."

Kristofer shrugged. "You came over here to tell me this? She's your wife; do as you please, but I'm sure she's going to know the difference," Kristofer nodded his head and smirked.

"They have strap-ons in the market that are made like yours," I paused, clearing my throat; I curled my lip, pointing in Kristofer's direction, "Penis."

He chuckled, "Them straps plastic, no matter how flesh-like they make them, it won't beat the real thing," Kristofer stood up, "Besides, what happens when you get the surgery? You still going through with that, right?" He raised his brow.

I threw my hands in the air and exhaled, "I'll figure it out as it comes. My actions before were deplorable, but I didn't realize how I'd feel after; It's wrong," I looked down. The truth is, I don't want my wife to get addicted to Kristofer's dick. I could feel the blood rush to my face.

Kristofer gripped my shoulder, "I get it, but that's something you should have thought before you paid me to have sex with her," he crossed his arms, "What caused you to rethink the plan? I warned you, but you begged me to continue!" Kristofer sat back on the bed, "The idea was absurd from the jump, but I'm telling you—that dildo won't cut it," he held his index and thumb close together, "Maybe you had a small chance if she hadn't had the real thing."

He was right; we made eye contact, and my eyes filled with water. I slumped over, sniffing, and whipped my face, "FUCK!" I screamed.

"You can't let this get to you like it is Essence will suspect something. You got this," Kristofer dapped my hand, "We got this," he smiled.

I was knee-deep in lies and couldn't afford to go back and forth like this. I would blow my cover if I got in my feelings every time Kristofer had sex with my wife. Plus, I needed him; Kristofer was right, I hate to admit—a strap-on was a bad idea now. Before I transitioned, no man had ever penetrated me to know the difference myself, but Sabrina reminded me every time we argued how much she missed having some real dick. I held my wrist up and looked at my watch; 10:45 *PM. Damn it! I know Essence is pissed,* I thought. I had already sent her to voicemail twice. I massaged my temples and paced the room, looking down.

"You straight?" Kristofer's eyes followed me as I paced back and forth.

I pinched the tip of my nose, "Take your clothes off; if I come in at this time empty-handed and don't give her any dick, she will let me have it." I remembered how Sabrina's attitude would change after we fuck; I decided it would be best for Kristofer to have sex with Essence tonight. "If ya'll have sex, she might overlook me being out this late and forgive me for not answering the phone."

Kristofer tilted his head, "Huh? Why am I taking my clothes off?" He creased his brows and slowly took his top off.

"I didn't leave wearing that, duh." I pointed at his clothes, "We need to exchange clothes so you can pretend to be me," I kicked off my shoes, unfastened my jeans, and handed them to him.

He shook his head, "Don't be so pushy," he undressed and handed me his clothing.

I pulled the cotton hoodie over my head and exited the hotel Detroit Riverside Casino. It was chilly; I cupped my hands and blew air, rubbing them together. I concocted a story for Kristofer to tell Essence about my whereabouts and climbed into the backseat of the Jeep. He seemed more focused on the radio than the cover story as he bobbed his head to the beat of *Overnight Celebrity* by Twista. As before, I wouldn't have the chance to watch them like on my honeymoon.

We arrived home within 20 minutes. Kristofer turned off the ignition and sat for another 10 minutes trying to calm my nerves. "If I stay in the truck longer, you are going to ruin your cover," he huffed, "Essence already looked out the window twice; I got this," Kristofer assured me.

Convinced Kristofer understood his story; I eased up. If he could only remember three simple words, attorney-client privilege, Essence should realize I couldn't share the details. I swallowed continuously, trying not to vomit; I wiped the sweat off my forehead and let out a long sigh. "Alright, man, gone before I change my mind," I hunched on the floor.

I heard muffled sounds from the house, unable to make out the words. From Essence's tone, she was pissed. I balled up my fist and hit the seat. "I can't believe I'm doing this to her," I whispered. Lying to Essence was unnerving. The yelling went on for another 15 minutes then the voices went silent. I lifted my head and peeped out the window, and the lights were off. I pressed the buttons on my watch—midnight. *It's starting,* I thought, shaking my head. I leaned on the door and closed my eyes, trying to think of everything but what was unfolding. The earliest I could have my surgery was December. My brother fucking my wife was the least of my worries; I needed to figure out a way to switch for an extended period without compromising my work and keep Essence from suspecting something was off. The plan had to be airtight.

I hadn't realized Kristofer had gotten back into the truck until I heard him crank the Jeep, startling me. The lights were out when he backed out of the driveway so he wouldn't wake Essence. I squinted and looked at the lights on the dash; it was 3:12 AM. Kristofer stopped at the end of the street and put the car in park. "Get out," he hopped in the passenger side. I walked around the Jeep and stretched my legs. It was uncomfortable crouching on the floor for three hours.

I closed the door and pulled off. "What happened? I heard her yelling, what did she say?" I looked at Kristofer; his head leaned back.

"She said what any newlywed would say if her husband left her for hours without warning." He glared at me and clenched his teeth before saying, "I didn't sign up for all this shit; being yelled at and having to console your wife," he shouted and closed his eyes again. "For now, on, unless you have an adequate plan to switch, I'm not doing it. That's my last time to be yelled at like I'm the husband."

I pressed my feet against the brake; we jerked forward. I held my arm against Kristofer's chest to prevent his head from slamming into the dashboard. "What the fuck you say?" My veins were throbbing in my neck.

He turned to me, "All I'm saying is the deal was for me to have sex with her, not get yelled at." He yawned and rubbed his eyes, "It's late, man; I need some sleep, and you have to get back before she wakes up."

I took my foot off the brake and hit 80 mph on the freeway. Calmly I looked at my brother. "Can you just highlight some of the things she said?"

He exhaled, "For starters, she was mad she couldn't reach you. In the future, answer the phone — you know, be a considerate husband, not a liar," he mumbled, then continued, "She is your wife, so as fucked up as your plan is, you got to at least act as though you care," we made eye contact.

Deceiving Essence will be more challenging than I thought. I stroked my beard and pressed my lips together. Although my decisions were selfish, there was a means to an end, and until I got there, I needed to keep Essence happy. A good plan will only work if my wife is happy. If I had to put in extra work to overcompensate for being deceitful, I was ready for the cause. I let out an exasperated sigh and pulled up to the casino.

I made it home in no time and could hear Essence snoring from the bedroom. I undressed in the kitchen and looked into the pantry for a garbage bag to get rid of the clothes I had on.

The floor creaked as I tiptoed down the hallway into the bedroom wearing only boxer briefs. These squeaky floors kept me in trouble when I was a teenager. I remember sneaking out of the house and getting caught by my mom; she was a light sleeper. Essence was a hard sleeper; you could practically use the pots and pans as drums and not wake her up.

I flinched from the wetness that soiled the sheets my hand landed in; disgusted, I curled my lip. Unsure if the moisture was from Essence or Kristofer, I closed my eyes, shaking the thought from my head. I stretched my arm to wrap it around Essence and pulled her closer. I whispered. "I'm sorry," and kissed her lips.

I was awakened by the constant taps on my shoulder. "Wake up!" Essence tapped me again. Blinking slowly, I parted my eyelids and looked at Essence, who was looking at the laptop. She smiled from ear to ear. I rubbed my eyes and sat up. "I found it," she turned the computer in my direction, shoving it in my face. I lowered my eyes, trying to focus on the bright screen. "What do you think about this one?" She pointed her finger at the 4-bedroom, three ½ -bath, European-style home in Farmington Hills. Her eyes sparkled as she eyed the pictures.

I sat up, "Let me take a look at it." I scrolled through the photos and admired the spiral staircase and all its amenities; the fully finished basement was my favorite. Essence's eyes were glued to the screen when I glanced at her. I clicked on the calendar and selected a timeslot to view the home before closing the laptop. "Get dressed; I made an appointment to see the house today," Essence's mouth dropped open. "Baby, you alright?" I smirked. She climbed onto her knees, crawled onto my lap, and wrapped her arms around my neck, grinning.

"Oh my God, I'm so excited," she playfully pressed her lips all over my face.

My palms gripped her soft ass. *Damn, I loved how it jiggles*, I thought. "Come on, go get ready, baby," I got out of bed and grabbed a pair of denim jeans and a polo sweatshirt from the closet.

"Let's shower together; we haven't done that since the honeymoon," Essence suggested walking into the bathroom.

I shifted from side to side, attempting to think of a response, "I got to make a couple of calls, babe; why don't you take yours since we have a small window to look at the house," I held my palms together and closed my eyes.

"Ah, okay, baby," she stuck her head out of the bathroom and pouted, "You got to make it up to me! Lucky, for you, I'm so excited about this house to make it an issue," she winked.

Soon as Essence was in the shower, I grabbed my cell and texted my brother: *I know you are tired of my impromptu favors, but I need you TONIGHT*. Happy wife, happy life was the idea, and I was willing to do almost anything to keep a smile on her face, including overnight switches, although it was getting too much for me. When we'd swap places, Essence had a glow I hadn't given her since the wedding. No sooner than I put the phone down, Kristofer replied: *I'm down!*

We made it to the property fifteen minutes earlier; the realtor was showing the home to another couple. Essence, entirely focused on her phone, swiped back and forth, looking at the rooms, "This house is exquisite, baby. I wonder how many agents submitted offers?"

"We can ask the realtor," I tilted my head back, sighing as I looked at the clock. "I hope their viewing ends soon."

"I hope they don't have many," she cut her eyes. "I want this house."

"Babe, we haven't looked at the place to know if you truly like it, the pictures are nice, but it's a million dollar investment; we can't take this lightly," I gripped her hand lightly.

"I know — but we will like it," she surmised.

I shook my head. Purchasing this home would be what's needed to keep her preoccupied. Essence found her niche in interior decorating like her mom. I smiled; this house was big enough to keep them both busy.

The realtor greeted us and invited us into the home. Essence's face beamed. I was impressed, too, "Looks like you both have something to think about," the realtor smiled, looking at our body language as she walked us through the home.

"We sure do," Essence and I said in agreement, "How many offers has this property received, and when is the deadline?"

"The house has received six offers, so if you're interested, I would suggest having your decision in by the end of the day," the realtor handed us the sellers' disclosures and her business card.

I grabbed the documents and pressed my lips together. "My wife and I will think it over," I smiled.

Essence's eyes sparkled on the ride home. We both loved the house, so I was going to place my bid. Finally, we arrived home; I inhaled and looked at my childhood home. I wasn't ready to give it up. Purchasing a new home would keep her occupied, but I needed to do more to pull the plan off; I needed to leave her father's firm. Working closely with Mr. Donaldson gave Essence access to my whereabouts, which would be damaging in the coming months.

"Babe, you know I will do anything to keep you happy, right," I said, reaching for her hand and squeezing it gently, "The house is gigantic; if our offer is accepted, I will need to work longer hours to afford the mortgage." I stroked her hair behind her ear.

She lowered her eyes, "Not forever," she leaned in closer, "It's our dream home, so I'm willing to do whatever it takes to help support our dream, short-term."

Setting the stage further, "Patience and understanding will go a long way," I exhaled. I could afford the place easily with the inheritance, but I needed wiggle room to accomplish my plan. I looked out the window, "I'm thinking 'bout switching firms; I didn't tell you yet because I was waiting for it to be official. TLG Law Group wants to meet with me. They want to offer me a position; it'll be a big promotion that could set us up for the future and help with this mortgage."

Essence covered her mouth, "Wow," she titled her head, "Does my dad know?"

I shook my head, "I haven't told him yet; I wanted to see how you'd feel first."

Essence took a deep breath, "My dad may be upset, but if that's what you feel is best for us, I think you should take it," she smiled.

"I know it's a lot at once," I looked Essence in the eye, "But first things first—let's place this bid," I grinned.

We placed our bid, and within 24 hours, the seller accepted. However, another offer would have outbid us if our agent didn't add the escalation clause to our bid. I could pull everything off; rubbing my hands together, I shared the news with Essence.

She twirled around the living room, "How long will it be before we close?" She gasped, plopping on the sofa, "I have to tell mama; she will be excited to help decorate."

Before answering, she exited the room to call her mom. I sat on the sofa and clutched my hands behind my head; I thought, *a few lies couldn't be so bad*. I would have it all the first of the year — a new house, a beautiful wife, and the body I always wanted.

Chapter Eleven

ESSENCE

"You can put those boxes over there," I pointed, directing the movers to the kitchen. I slumped my back against the living room wall, looking at the million boxes that filled the room.

"Baby, that wall can hold itself up," my mother sounded upbeat. "This is exciting, honey. Once the movers are finished moving you, we can start decorating. Have you and Christian decided on color schemes?"

"Color schemes," barely standing up, I rested my weight on one leg. "No, we haven't, but he said he's cool with whatever I decide."

"Really?" Sounding enthused, "Well, show me around this castle." Throwing her head back, we walked from room to room. As my mom peeked into the rooms, she jotted down notes. Her face beamed as she walked into the next room, "This would be perfect for a nursery," my mother cooed, cutting her eyes in my direction.

"I know," my eyes widened as I stared into the room, imagining it filled with a crib.

"Have you and Christian started talking about having kids?" My mother raised her brows, waiting on my response.

"I mean, not really. Christian evades the subject. I honestly don't know if he wants kids," I crossed my arms, sighing.

"Honey, I live by the philosophy that you must ask for forgiveness, not permission." She spoke rapidly, "Since you have free reign to decorate, make this the nursery. We can place one of those do not enter signs on the door and have a big reveal when it's finished."

My eyes widened as I bit my lip, "You think so? I mean, that's assertive."

"YES! By the time he sets his eyes on this room, he's going to want twins," she squeezed my hand gently.

"Alright, let's do it!" I spun around, "Let's continue seeing the rest of the house and talk next steps."

Christian stepped over the trail of boxes leading from the door, "Damn baby, I could hardly get up the stairs." He grinned at me, "You still excited about the house?"

Cutting my eyes in his direction, I placed the back of my hand on my forehead. "Yes, in a few days, the boxes will be empty, and the real fun will start." I leaned forward and pressed my lips on his, "I won't front though, I am tired, boss," we giggled, "I was thinking, when I finish decorating, we should have a housewarming."

Christian grabbed my foot, gently rubbing them with his strong hands. "You were thinking, huh?"

Nodding, I moaned, "Yes, what do you think of that?"

"Whatever you want," he gripped me by my ankles, dragging me closer to the bottom of the bed, and sucked on my toes.

"Baby, what are you doing?"

He unbuckled my pants, "What does it look like I am doing?" He gestured for me to lift my hips as he slid my pants off. He licked his lips and got on his knees. "I have been thinking about your pussy all damn day, baby. You gone feed me?"

I hummed, biting my bottom lip, "Yes, baby," I spread my legs so he could have a better view. There were two things undeniable about Mr. Powell: He could eat the hell out of a pussy, and that DICK OMG, my husband was blessed; I hit the jackpot!

Christian fluttered his tongue up and down my clit, slurping. His stiffened finger slid into my vagina, giving me a dual sensation. My nipples were erect, and I rubbed them before he swatted my hands out of the way so he could massage them to my climax. My lips quivered as I thrust my hips up and down against his face. Christian moaned, "This my pussy," he mumbled.

"This is YOUR pussy," my legs shook uncontrollably, "I'M CUMMING," I shouted from the top of my lungs.

He wiped his mouth with the back of his hands, swallowing hard, "I love you, baby," he crawled up to me, parting my lips and kissing me deeply. "Want me to run you a shower?"

"Yes, please," I hurried out of bed and grabbed a silk teddy from the open box, "Are you joining me?"

"Absolutely, but I have to work late tonight, so we have to make it quick," he undid his belt buckle. His penis was massive; it held up his shirt.

I grinned, crawling toward him, "I'm sure you can make time," I stuck my tongue out, licking the tip.

He flinched, stepping back, "Whoa, what are you doing?"

"Come on, baby; you never let me. What's the matter?" I questioned, sticking my tongue out and licking the tip again.

Christian's knees buckled as he moaned, "You got to stop," he pleaded.

"You don't want me to stop," I grabbed his penis, wrapping my lips around him. I could feel his dick jump in my mouth as it pulsated. He leaned his head back and moaned louder. His hands gripped the back of my neck. *For this to be my first time sucking dick, it's not so bad,* I thought to myself. Following the motion of Christian's thrust, I sucked his penis slowly and jerked him off simultaneously.

"Ahhh, baby…baby…baby," he groaned as he stumbled backward. I watched the cum squirt and pour all over the floor. Then, reaching down, he picked me up, and I wrapped my legs around his waist, kissing him passionately.

He carried me to the bathroom, placing me on the sink to completely undress me. Mirroring him, I took off my t-shirt and waited for his next move. Gently picking me up, he carried me over to the shower, legs still wrapped around him, he pushed my back against the wall, and I felt his hardened dick enter me. Moaning in harmony, we continued making love in the shower. My legs were wobbly by the time we finished. I sat on the bed and rubbed baby oil on my legs as I watched Christian dress.

I grabbed my lingerie, admiring his physique, "How late will you be working?" I asked curiously.

He looked at his watch and made eye contact, "I shouldn't be much longer, I hope. After those rounds, I'm sure you will be asleep when I make it home," he smirked.

I stretched my arms, letting out a yarn, "You're right. I will be sleeping pretty soon. Tomorrow, I need all my energy to sort through boxes and organize things as much as possible."

Christian leaned over, kissing my forehead softly, "I'll try not to be too long."

Moments after hearing the door shut, I was knocked out. The light from the blinds shinned on my face. My eyelids slowly blinked as I adjusted to the darkness.

Chapter Twelve

CHRISTIAN

The coming weeks went by smoother than butter. Essence and her mother were preoccupied with decorating the new home. Finally, I had a perfect schedule for Kristofer and me to switch places when Essence got that itch and wanted some dick. You'd think I made a bid with the devil, or my guardian angel was looking out for me. At this rate, if my luck doesn't run out, I don't see what could go wrong.

Essence grew increasingly happy the week of our housewarming. The decrease in sex didn't alter her mood either, considering the house had her hands tied with finalizing the last details of our event. The morning of the party, she removed the do not enter sign from the room she kept locked and placed a bright red giant bow on the door. This room must be why she's excited; I smiled. I tiptoed behind Essence and wrapped my arms around her waist, "I see why you've been in such a good mood this week. Is it my man cave?" I questioned jokingly.

She hummed, "Could be; you just have to wait and see," pressing her lips against mine. "Hurry up and get changed."

I was impressed by how good Essence and her mother decorated the house. The moment our guests stepped through the door, they oohed and aahed wide-eyed turning their heads, admiring the interior. Essence called the guest to the living room two hours into the gathering. "I am so glad you all decided to come and celebrate the new home with Christian and me. However, the evening will not be complete until you join me to reveal a surprise I put together for Christian." She walked through the small opening between the guest and up the stairs signaling me with her hand, "Baby, follow me; To prevent any hazards, we can't have all the guests up here at once, but if my parents and Madison can join us. I will allow the rest of you to take a look afterward."

"What is it?" I mouthed to my mother-in-law, who grinned from ear to ear. I stood next to Essence, who held the scissors.

"Thank you for taking the first step in building a legacy by purchasing our first home." She paused and cleared her throat, "I put a lot of thought into this last room, babe. I know you want a man cave," Essence waited again, building the suspense; she cut the bow, "It's not a man cave," she twisted the knobbed and swung the door open, "It's a nursery," she beamed looking at her design.

My mouth gapped open as my eyes bulged. I stood frozen in place, unsure of what to say. My father-in-law read my facial expression and could see I was not excited as she was. And, it was even more apparent Essence had not seen my disappointment yet. He held his champagne flute in the air to prevent this evening from becoming a disaster. "Let us all raise our champagne glasses and make a toast; to new beginnings," he walked towards Essence, clinking her flute against his and sipping the champagne.

Mrs. Donaldson shuffled towards me. "What's wrong, don't you like the nursery? It was Essence's idea to pick out gender-neutral colors," the corners of her mouth curled up as she sipped more champagne.

"It's…not what I expected," I scratched my head, cracking a half smile with wrinkled brows, "It's nice, though." I sipped from my flute.

I made my way downstairs with the guest and sat on the sofa, "You all can take a look if you like," I pointed towards the staircase.

As the guests made their way up and down the stairs to view the nursery, conversations shifted from our glamourous new home to Essence and me having a baby, and I grew increasingly uncomfortable.

We seriously needed to talk. But, glancing at my wife, I thought tonight was not the time from how Essence and Madison slurred their speech, laughing hysterically and catching up with each other.

"Babe, you've been quiet since the housewarming. Did you have a good time?" She sat the plate of seared steak, redskin potatoes, and asparagus in front of me as she walked back to the stove to fix her plate.

"Yeah, I enjoyed everything up until you blind-sided me with that nursey," I picked up my steak knife, cut into the New York strip, and poured a tad of Heinz 57 across the beef.

"I thought you would like it," she walked back to the table and sat across from me with her baked chicken and sides. "I try to talk to you about kids often, and since we have so much space, I thought the surprise would be well received."

"There are better ways to discuss kids. It was awkward for me to correct YOUR family and tell them WE aren't pregnant and that I don't know when you will be," my eyes narrowed as I put my knife down on the table, crossing my arms.

"So, when is it a good time, CHRISTIAN?" She screamed, "I seem to pick the wrong times, so YOU tell me when we should talk about it," she poked at her potatoes before putting her fork down.

Essence's eyes filled with water and a tear trickled down her cheek. My heart palpated, and I looked down, breaking eye contact, and shrugged a shoulder. "I know you want to have kids, baby; I want to give them to you," wiping her tears, "I hesitated before choosing my next words, "I can't have kids."

Essence tilted her head, "Wait, what?" She threw her palms in the air, scooted her chair away from the table, crossed her arms, and stood in front of me, "What are you talking about, Christian?" her brows furrowed.

I held her hand firmly, "I went and got checked, and the doctor told me I'm not able to have kids," I covered my face.

She stepped back, glancing sideways, "When was your appointment, and why am I first hearing about this? I am your WIFE; I should have known way before today."

My shoulders slumped as the lies fell from my lips effortlessly, "Before I met you," she gasped and covered her mouth as I continued, "I was diagnosed with undescended testicles."

Her hand waved dismissively, and she pressed her lips together, taking a deep breath. Essence shook her head, "So you knew this BEFORE we got married? Now, I'm no attorney, so correct me if I'm wrong, but isn't that grounds for an annulment in Michigan?"

"I'm not a divorce attorney," I said, twisting my ring; my words stuttered, "Let's talk about this. I love you; this was hard for me to tell you I can't give you what you want."

"Christian, my disappointment is not about your inability to give me kids; it's your DECEIT," her eyes rolled as she let out an exasperated sigh. Essence placed her palm against her forehead, rubbing her stomach. Her breath quickened; she ran into the bathroom and quickly shut the door.

She stayed in the bathroom for the next few minutes as I sat outside listening to her vomit, "Baby, I'm so sorry," I spoke after she flushed the toilet and ran some water.

The door swung open; she wiped her mouth, "I don't have the stomach to talk tonight, but we will continue this conversation tomorrow," she said, walking past me and upstairs, "This conversation makes me sick."

I stared out the kitchen window the next day, thinking what Essence would say as I stirred honey into her ginger tea. The sweat beaded my forehead. Would she really file for an annulment? I wiped my head and headed upstairs. "I made you some tea to settle your stomach," I placed the mug on the nightstand and sat next to her, "We have a lot to discuss," before I could finish my sentence, she interrupted me and sat up in the bed.

"I did a lot of thinking last night. I am ANGRY that you lied to me, but I'm even more disappointed in myself. I was naive to marry you without having serious conversations about finances, health, and building a family. Sometimes, I feel like I don't even know you." Essence grabbed the tea and blew her breath over it before taking a sip, "I circled the thought of filing for an annulment, but I married you because I love you, so I'm choosing my marriage, and hopefully, we can adopt kids in the future. But, I ASSURE you, I will file for a divorce if you EVER lie to me again!"

She eyed me intensively, waiting for my response, "Baby, I will do anything to earn your trust, and I'm open to adoption," the corners of my mouth curled as I wrapped my arms around her.

My marriage felt like a game of tug-of-war. After I told Essence I couldn't have children, she suggested we see a therapist. I agreed to it as long as the shrink was a man. Additionally, Essence began to complain more that I was always working late and disappeared without explanation.

For weeks, I've methodically planned how Kristofer and I would trade places so that I could have surgery. I stopped working for Bradley-Dickerson Law Firm and freelanced at a different firm until my interview with TLG Law Group. The caseload I had left me inundated with work; I was the first chair working on a criminal case. Essence demanded that we have a date night, a suggestion the therapist provided us. Unfortunately, there needed to be more time in the day to sleep, eat, work, trade places, and find time for date nights.

On top of that, Essence wasn't getting any dick because I was jealous that Kristofer was constantly having sex with her, and I had to hear about it the next day. Our sex life was like night and day. I would give Essence every excuse from being busy, under the weather, not in the mood, or tired, but she was persistent. Eventually, to prevent an even bigger problem, I gave in to her request. After I agreed to a date night, Essence planned it immediately, giving me no time to go over the details with

Kristofer, something he had previously complained of. I had reservations about switching places with Kristofer, and Essence scolded me the next day about *my* behavior. Kristofer got so drunk that he stumbled all over the place and was obnoxiously rude in public. His behavior was alarming when Essence re-played the night to me; I closed my eyes and placed my hand over my mouth, embarrassed by the details. I was even more stunned to find out she still had sex and enjoyed it, considering how pissed she was.

To avoid a catastrophe while I was gone, I paid Kristofer top dollar to convince him not to drink more than two drinks whenever they were out and to ensure he kept things scripted. It was such a vulnerable feeling knowing my marriage was hang-ing on by a thread. One wrong move and the plan would blow up in smoke.

The plot to deceive my wife was not the most challenging part of this charade; it was teaching Kristofer law. All he knew about the law was breaking it. The last month I've come home late so I could meet up with Kristofer to condense years of law school so he would understand legal terms, how to file motions, and master my day-to-day tasks to pass as me in my absence. Kristofer seemed as close to legit after rehearsing nightly that our plan was fools' proof as long as we played our parts.

The involuntary fidgeting was a dead giveaway I had a lot on my mind. As much as I attempted to act normal, Essence could see the worry on my face. My stomach was doing cartwheels. I placed my hand on my stomach to ease my nerves as I rubbed it in a circular motion. I took a long breath and wiped the water that was beading on my forehead.

"What's the matter? You've been poking at your Cesar salad since the server brought it. Are you nervous about interviewing with TLG Law Group?" Essence asked, narrowing her eyes as she reached across the table, gripping my hand. Then, finally, she let go and picked up the white tablecloth to rub her hand across the fabric, "Ugh, Christian, your hand is clammy. Babe, you will be fine," she replied with the corners of her mouth curled, "Don't stress yourself out. They're poaching YOU, remember?"

My eyes shifted to the tavern's window as I watched the pedestrians cross the street. I had lied and told Essence they sought me, but I applied to get from under her father. Also, I was interviewing with the firm the day before surgery to have a small window to swap places with Kristofer smoothly.

"I'm nervous; I can't help it," I said, cracking a half smile, "Thank you for meeting me for lunch. I don't have much of an appetite, though," I said, putting my fork down on the napkin after poking at my food for the last five minutes. I tugged at my tie and cleared my throat as I watched Essence chew on the chicken parmesan she ordered. The thought of her digging her nails into Kristofer as she made love to him instantly entered my mind. *There couldn't be a better time for my mind to wander*, I thought to myself. I shook my head back and forth and shut my eyes tight to get the thought out. Then, finally, I exhaled, "Babe, I'll be home late again. I have a deposition to prepare for before my trip."

Essence dropped her knife and fork, causing a loud clink as the metal clashed against the white ceramic plate, "What's late, Christian?" she scoffed, "Can you use the office at home to prepare? You've come home late for the last month."

"You know it's hard for me to focus knowing your fine ass is a floor above me," I smirked, raising my eyebrows.

Essence rolled her eyes, grabbed the napkin from the table to wipe her mouth, and mumbled, "I can't tell."

I grabbed the glass of water and placed it in front of me, narrowing my eyes, "What's that supposed to mean?" I asked, gripping the glass. Of course, I knew what Essence meant precisely, but I was going to act naive.

"I've practically walked around naked or in a teddy, and you never made a move or looked in my direction Christian," she said, crossing her arms.

"If you know I'm trying to work, why would you tease me like that?" I scoffed, gaslighting her. I didn't want to rile Essence, but her attitude made it impossible not to.

"Really? You know what?" she said, stopping in the middle of her sentence, "Let's finish lunch. I don't have the energy to go back and forth with you, Christian."

I took long blinks and made eye contact, "I have a lot on my plate. But I promise things will get better soon," I said, reaching over to grab her hand.

We both sat in silence for the remainder of our lunch date. I hate seeing the dissatisfaction in Essence's eyes. One thing I'm looking forward to is life after surgery because I needed balance. Essence didn't have this in mind when we decided to marry each other. Having surgery would be the giant step I needed to get us back on track. There would be no need to swap places or work long hours. Instead, I could be focused entirely on her. I don't know what I did to deserve a woman as great as she. I tested our love regularly, but I am prepared to give her everything to make things up to her.

Before the waiter could come back with the receipt, Essence was already putting on her peacoat. I could tell Essence was aggravated by the half-hug she gave me on her way out of the restaurant. The plan was for Kristofer and me to swap places tonight, but I didn't want to leave on bad terms. Who knows what could happen in surgery? So, while it was essential to stick to the plan, I had to make a judgment call and adjust plans slightly. Every decision I made to keep my secret wouldn't be worth it if something happened to me in surgery. On the other hand, I didn't want to upset her, so I decided to spend my last night with Essence before I left tomorrow; tomorrow would be a better day.

I made it back to the office and contacted Kristofer to let him know about the sudden change in plans. It was always his idea that we traded places after work instead of me going home. Shortly into the conversation, I could hear the disturbance in his voice as he sighed heavily. He vehemently suggested we stick to the original plan to avoid any mishaps. I wish he would be more understanding, considering I was having surgery tomorrow. Of course, any husband would want to spend time with his wife before surgery, but the way he yelled, "IT'S YOUR FU-NERAL," before hanging up the phone, made it crystal clear he wasn't feeling the slight change in our plans. Kristofer's reactions made me uneasy. *Why does he care so much?* I thought. I had way too many things on my mind, and worrying about Kristofer was extra. If I never doubted swapping places with him before, I for damn sure was now. My surgery was too close for the plan to start unraveling.

The conversation between Kristofer and me wasn't sitting well with me, so I left work early, and instead of going home, I headed to the Detroit Riverside Casino to gauge my brother's mood. We both needed a good mental headspace to pull off the plan.

I reached room 233 and slumped my back against the adjacent wall before knocking. The sweat was falling uncontrollably from my forehead; you'd think I ran from the car to the room, as I panted out of breath. I removed my handkerchief from my suit jacket and pressed it against my face. I cleared my throat, walked in front of the door, and knocked on Kristofer's suite.

"Yo, it's me. Open up," I shouted, hitting my fist against the wood. A few seconds went by before the door swung open. Kristofer wiped his narrow eyes and stepped aside in the darkened room. The TV was on, but there was no sound. "You sleep, bro?" I questioned as I walked into the room and leaned against the dresser.

Kristofer walked towards the room after locking the door and plopped down on the bed. I fiddled with the keys and cracked a smile, "You ready for tomorrow?" I asked.

"Why are you here?" he lowered his eyes, "Aren't you supposed to be at home packing for your trip?" Kristofer leaned back on the bed.

"I wanted to check and see if you were alright; you seemed upset by me changing plans," I sat next to him and patted him on the back.

He grinned, "I'm not upset; I just think it's stupid, but I get it." Then, he lit a cigarette and took a puff; he changed the subject, "How are you feeling about surgery?"

I smiled, "I'm excited; I can't believe it's really about to happen. I waited so long," I stood up and sat on the dresser to escape the direct smoke.

"Yeah, I can't imagine. So how does it go? Do you get to pick out the size?" he leaned toward me.

I pressed my lips together and shook my head, "No, it's a process; they take skin graft tissue from my thighs and arms. It's a three-part process spanning over a year and a half."

Kristofer furrowed his brow, "What? So, you plan on this reoccurring to finish the process?" He stood up and scratched his head, "I can't stay around and live up in a hotel until you're done with that," he sat back down and put out his cigarette butt.

"You don't have to. I will give you the old house to live in," I smiled at the thought of Kristofer agreeing to stick around.

Kristofer pressed his lips, "The new house is nice," he smirked, "You must be swimming in cash," he scoffed.

"Well, if you want a new house, we can discuss adding that as part of the agreement; I am sure we can work out the details if you stay." I got up and sat next to him.

He shook his head. "I'll have to think about that, Christian. After this, I planned to get away from here for a while."

"Just think about it," I got up and headed to the door. "I need to get going; I'll be here early in the morning, so be ready," I closed the door.

I grinned, driving home and thinking of the possibility of Kristofer sticking around to complete my female to male transition. Finally, I made it home; all the lights were out. I poured a glass of cognac and grabbed the plate of food Essence left in the refrigerator for me; I exhaled. *Maybe I should have let Kristofer come tonight since she was already asleep;* I thought, it was my last night, we should be making love while I confessed my love to her— but sleep seemed like the agenda since I had a big day ahead of me.

Chapter Thirteen

ESSENCE

I left the Detroit Riverside casino and hit the freeway at 100mph, weaving in and out of traffic. I gripped the steering wheel, trying to stop my hands from shaking uncontrollably, "I CAN'T BELIEVE THIS SHIT," I screamed, driving toward Madison's Southfield home. My eyes darted to the seat. When I heard the muffled sound from my cellular phone vibrating against the leather. "Don't fucking call me EVER," I screamed into the phone and swiftly hit the end button disconnecting, not allowing a chance for Christian to respond.

I arrived at Madison's house and banged on the door with my fist. The neighbors' porch lights flicked on one by one as I awakened them by the loud thuds the wooden door made. The faintness in Madison's footsteps grew louder the closer she reached the door, "Who is it?" she shouted before the blinds moved back and forth. Then, finally, Madison swung the door wide open. "What the hell is wrong with you?" she snapped as she rubbed her hand against her eye, "It's after 4:00 AM; what are you doing here?" she asked, and slipped backward when I ran past her to get inside the house before she shut the door.

My lips quivered; I paced back and forth in her living room with my hands balled into a fist. "Christian, I caught him cheating," I sobbed hysterically, falling to my knees.

Madison walked towards me, placed her arm around my hunched back, and rubbed gently, trying to soothe me. She waited a few minutes before speaking to allow me time to control myself, "What happened, Essence?" she questioned with a concerned tone.

I leaned up and wiped my face with the back of my hand. "I followed Christian to the hotel and caught him inside the room with another man," I said as water streamed from the corners of my eyes.

"A MAN! Are you sure?" she shrieked, "Wait, what made you follow him to a hotel?" She asked with one brow raised. She sat down next to me on the floor with a puzzled expression. I hadn't spoken to Madison about my suspicions of Christian because I feared embarrassment or hearing an "I told you so." After all, she always felt he and I was rushing the marriage.

I took a long, exasperated breath and let out a sigh. "He's been acting strange the last few months, and he's been coming home later and later, and when I'd confront him, he'd say he was working. Christian no longer works with my dad, so I can't ask what he's up to as I did before. Plus, we stopped having sex COMPLETELY. He's extremely affectionate one minute and cold the next; I don't know who he is anymore. It feels like Christian is a stranger at times." I shrugged my shoulders and continued, "All of this started happening after he told me he couldn't have kids," I said, wiping the tears from my eyes.

Madison placed her hand over her mouth, "Girl, hell no, I can't believe this shit!" She said with lowered eyebrows, "What did he say when you saw him?" Madison interrogated and stared me in the eyes.

I ran my hands through my untamed hair. "He didn't say shit! As soon as I saw him, I walked back out of the room and left his ass there. I feel stupid! I knew something was going on, but I never thought I'd see that shit," I said with veins throbbing in my neck. My purse started vibrating; I reached down inside then rolled my eyes, "He won't stop fucking calling me," I said, throwing the phone across the room and striking the wall.

"You got to talk to him to see what he has to say. Shit, I'll talk to him. You know I'm down to do whatever you want to do," Madison said, standing up to walk across the room to grab my cracked phone on the floor and hand it to me.

Madison walked towards her room, "Why does this always happen to me? First Roderick and now Christian?" I asked, plopping down on the edge of her bed and poking my bottom lip out. Madison sat down next to me; her face was distressed. She held me silently; I laid my head on her shoulder and wept. Finally, Madison lifted my head, wiped the tears from my face, and pressed her lips against my forehead. The tenderness she displayed had me think back to when we shared a kiss. We both made steady eye contact for a few moments until I shut my eyes and leaned forward, grabbing the nape of her neck and pressing my lips against hers.

I could feel Madison tense up, and her head jerked back. I opened my eyes and saw her eyes budge, "What are you doing?" Madison asked as she stood up from the bed, glaring down at me.

I stood up from the bed and looked away as I buried my face in my hands, embarrassed that she refused my kiss. "I'm sorry; I don't know what came over me. Maybe I should go," I replied. I snatched my purse and placed it over my shoulder, heading towards her bedroom door. I felt the warmth of Madison's skin as she reached out and grabbed my wrist.

"No, you're too worked up to be driving," she replied, pulling me back and stopping me dead in my tracks.

"No. I should go," I said, pulling my wrist back and nodding in disagreement, feeling ashamed and rejected.

"No, stay," Madison said, walking ahead of me and standing in front of the door. There was a sudden change in her demeanor as she pulled me closer to her. "I want you to stay," she said, walking closer to me. Madison stared me deep in the eyes before wrapping her arms around my waist. She pressed her lips against mine, parting my mouth with her tongue. She kissed me softly and sensually; it was very intense.

Our kiss was interrupted as Madison let go of our embrace and looked me in the eyes again. I smiled and bit my lip, watching as she pulled the string of her robe open to reveal her naked body. Her skin looked soft; it glowed from the dim light against her body. My heart started pulsating against my chest, and my breath quickened as my eyes traced her curvy body. Madison's hands guided me, and I anxiously obeyed her as she lifted my arms, taking off my top. Her index finger slid into the top of my pants, and she aggressively pulled me closer. She whispered faintly into my ear. "I want you." Her warm breath tickled my ear, and I felt the hairs on the back of my neck stand as she unfastened my bra; Madison turned me on.

She grabbed my pants and underwear, yanking them down from around my waist, then cupped my breasts in her hands and pressed them together, licking my erect nipples. I flinched from the warmth of her mouth. *Her familiar touch was foreign,* I thought as her hand glided between my legs to massage my clitoris. Repeatedly, I fluttered from the pleasure, "You feel so good," I moaned.

She pushed me gently, and I stumbled backward and fell on the bed as I watched her crawl from the bottom. Madison narrowed the slits of her eyes as she stared at me seductively. Her hands glided against my skin, spreading my legs open so she could position herself between them. She pressed her body against mine and ran her lips across my neck, faintly biting me before she slid her fingers in and out of my moist opening. I closed my eyes and dug my nails into her skin as I arched my back and gripped her shoulders. Madison turned me on even more when I opened my eyes and watched her lick my nectar from her fingertips.

"I've been wanting you for so long," she admitted as she whispered before she slid back down between my legs, placing me into her mouth. Initially, I lay there rigid, completely taken aback by what was happening. *I'm fucking my best friend*, I thought, but that thought promptly vanished when her hands grip my ass.

The palm of my hands caressed my nipples, and I began to grind my hips back and forth while she sucked and flicked her tongue across my clitoris. My body started to tense up, and my legs twitched as I held Madison's head in place. Finally, I could feel myself climax. "I'm cumming," I moaned in ecstasy. Then, gasping for air, I leaned forward and kissed her, gently tasting the bittersweetness from her lips.

Madison wiped her mouth with the back of her arm and smiled at me, collapsing onto the bed. I crawled on her, straddling her waist, and felt her moistness. I rubbed my vagina against hers. Her hands gripped my ass tightly as she moved her hips up and down. The feeling of her stiffened clitoris made me arch my back, matching the rhythm she made with her body while grinding against each other. I watched Madison tilt her head back. "Don't stop," she panted. I thrust my hips up and down and felt myself cum for the second time.

Sweaty and out of breath, I lay beside her. *What have I done? I am as guilty as Christian*, I thought as she wrapped her arm around me, spooning. I waited until she was fast asleep and slid away from her embrace. I thought back to Christian and what he could have been doing at the hotel. I am a hypocrite! My eyes filled with water, and I blinked away the tears as I balled myself up, dozing off feeling ashamed.

The crackling sound of hot grease and the smell of fried eggs and pork woke me out of my sleep. I squinted my eyes and yarned; I sat up and slid my back against the cool wooden head-board. My eyes scanned her room, looking for an alarm clock. "What time is it?" I asked Madison as she walked into the bed-room with a breakfast plate and a coffee mug.

"It's a little after 8:00 AM; are you hungry?" She handed me the plate and exited the bedroom. I took two bites of the toast and fried eggs, hardly swallowing; I felt my mouth salivate. The salty taste that filled my mouth caused me to clench my jaw. I got up from the bed and ran into the bathroom just in time to lean over the toilet. My stomach contracted, forcing the chewed-up eggs to spew out, landing in the toilet. Madison ran into the bathroom with her lip curled. "Are you alright?" she asked.

My knees felt weak. I got up and walked to the sink to turn on the water. I cupped my hands, splashing the cold water against my face, leaned over the sink, opened my mouth under the stream of water, and took a sip. "I'm alright. I guess my nerves are a bit jacked up this morning." I walked back into the room and sat on the bed, staring at the plate of food.

Madison sat down next to me, tilted her head, and pressed her lips together. She sat silently for a minute with a fixed gaze. "Do you think you're pregnant?" she questioned.

I sat there frozen, staring at the wall. Then, the feeling of Madison's cold hands sliding into my clammy palms broke my train of thought. "The thought never crossed my mind. Christian and I hadn't touched each other within the last few weeks, and he told me he can't have kids recently, remember?"

"Well, when was your last period," Madison cut me off.

I squinted my eyes, "I'm about a week late," I said as I released an exasperated sigh. "It could just be stress, though," I shrugged.

Madison's mouth gapped open. "Wow, so when do you plan on taking a test?" She stared at me with wide eyes and raised eyebrows. She reached into her pocket and handed me my shattered cell phone, "Your phone hasn't stopped ringing."

I looked at the missed phone calls from Christian and text messages. I opened the texts and read them silently. My eyes bulged, "WHAT?" I shouted in disbelief as I jumped out of bed, looking for my clothes.

"What's wrong? What did he say?" Madison stood up and handed me my shirt on the floor next to her.

"Girl, Christian claims I saw him at the hotel with his brother. Can you believe this shit?" I put on my clothes and read more of his messages.

Madison folded her arms across her chest. "I thought you said he's the only child?" She scratched her head, "Don't fall for that bullshit," she growled.

"He did tell me that." I scanned the messages. My eyes widened. I looked at a photo of Christian and his brother he sent, twins. I dropped the phone, mouth gaping open in disbelief. "I have to go," I said, reaching for my purse.

Madison stood up and walked in front of the bedroom door, blocking me, "This doesn't make sense. How do you know Christian is not lying? He lied and said he was an only child, and now suddenly he has a brother?" She placed her hands on her waist.

I rolled my eyes, picked up the phone from the floor, and sighed. I showed Madison the picture I'd received. "See, look," I placed my finger on the photo in my phone of Christian and his twin. "That's why I need to go talk to him to see what's going on." I placed my phone into my purse and shoved Madison out the way.

"You're just going to leave? We haven't even gotten a chance to talk about last night. Stay," she said as she clutched my hand; narrowing her eyes; she pleaded.

"Madison, I have to go. I promise we can talk about this later," I said, snatching my hand away from her grip and tapping my feet against the floor as I grew impatient with her.

She shook her head. "This isn't fair! You come over, make love to me, and leave without discussing it. Tell me that you didn't feel anything last night. I know you did," Madison pouted; water rushed from the corners of her eyes.

"What do you want me to say, Madison? I'm married, plus I might be pregnant, so whether you like it or not, I have to go and talk to my HUSBAND and see what's going on. We can talk later," I said, raising my voice and forcing my way around her, not looking back as the door slammed behind me.

When I pulled up to our Farmington Hills estate, no lights were on. Christian parked his car in the driveway, so I knew he was home. I let myself in and hollered for Christian as I ran up the spiral staircase. Christian was slumped over on the floor with bloodshot eyes when I walked into the room. He stood up, wearing plaid pajama pants, and ran around to me. "I'm so sorry, baby," he dropped to the floor in front of me and wrapped his arms around my waist.

Half of me wanted to console him and tell him everything would be alright. But the other half made me want to slap the shit out of him; I've never seen him cry like this, even at his mother's funeral. Yes, he was hurt, but his actions caused his pain. I've been 100 percent honest with him from the beginning, so I cannot fathom why he'd lie to me; he had no reason to be dishonest. I peeled his arms from around my waist, "Stop!" I screamed, stepping away from him. I was angry; one for all his lies and the second knowing that I betrayed him, and I was fearful of exposing my secret. "Christian, you're hurt because of you. Why would you lie to me? It makes me question everything about you," I said, glaring down at him.

"Baby, I know I was wrong, and I can't apologize enough for it," he stood up and held my hands. "I am truly sorry – you have to believe me."

I snatched my hands away and walked over to the bed, "I want to know why you lied." I held my palm in front of him. "Before you say anything, if you lie to me again, I'm walking out that door, and we are getting divorced."

Christian looked away and hesitated before speaking, "A few years ago, before my brother joined the Army, he and I fought. After that, he said he hated me and didn't want anything to do with me or our mom anymore. I thought he was dead when he didn't show up for the funeral. It's been years since I heard from him."

"Why? What was so bad that he didn't want to have a relationship with both of you?" I crossed my arms over my chest.

Christian shrugged his shoulders and shook his head. "I don't know," he responded, looking away from me. I twisted my mouth and stormed down the stairs, Christian on my heels, "Where are you going?" he followed me into his office.

"I don't believe you," I said as I pointed my finger in his face. The more he opened his mouth, the less I believed him. "I bet all the answers I want to know are in this filing cabinet you keep locked," I reached over, pulling on the drawers, "You spend countless hours in here, doors locked; I know you're not working. So, what are you hiding?" I yelled and opened his desk drawer and started moving papers around, searching for the keys.

"Baby, please stop! Nothing is in these cabinets but files for my clients," Christian pushed the doors closed that I opened. "When we were kids, he was jealous of how close my mother and I were. He thought she favored me. Don't you think it hurts me to know the only living family I know, does not want to ever speak to me, is my twin brother? Shit, my identical brother? Don't you think that bothers me?"

I sat down in the desk chair and rested my chin on my hand as I watched him pace the foyer. "I'm sorry to hear that, but it doesn't erase anything. I'm your wife; there shouldn't be secrets between us," I said as I got up, walked over to him, and looked him in the eyes swallowing hard.

"I know, and I'm willing to do whatever it takes to make this up to you," Christian said with his hands pressed in a steeple.

"Good. I want to meet your brother; what's his name?" I crease my brows.

"Kristofer," he looked at me and cracked a fake smile.

"Invite him over for dinner Friday. That should give you time to talk and fix whatever issue you all have." I patted him on the shoulder and walked up the stairs to shower. I was starting to question my judge of character, and Christian's vague explanation didn't make me feel any better, so I was going to try to get to the bottom of it myself.

The past few days had been a rollercoaster of events. Christian sent me flowers; he was home on time and even agreed to see a female marriage counselor. He had a long way to go to earn my trust, but I liked the effort thus far. I was anxious to know the outcome of our marriage, especially if it turned out I was pregnant. I'd avoided taking a pregnancy test because I was partly scared of the results and wanted to get past the dinner first. Madison called my phone multiple times after I walked out on her, and I felt terrible for it, but I didn't need any added drama. I planned on returning her calls but resolving my issues was more important than speaking about our minor indiscretion that shouldn't have happened.

The aroma of herb-roasted lamb chops and buttery garlic mashed potatoes filled the kitchen. I sat at the table and waited patiently for Christian and his twin brother, Kristofer, to arrive. I saw the lights of Christian's Jeep beam against the wall from his headlights as he pulled into the driveway. My stomach was in knots. I took a deep breath and opened the door swallowing hard. The resemblance between my husband and Kristofer was striking. "Wow," I said, speechless, and I stood eyeing Christian and his brother up and down. "Isn't this something identical," I said, reaching over and embracing Kristofer with a tight hug. After a few seconds, I let go. "Come on in," I said, stepping aside and welcoming Kristofer into our home, "Christian can show you where to hang your things. We have so much catching up to do."

I noticed Kristofer eyes darted in the direction of Christian with a fixed stare. "It's a lot of things I'm sure he didn't tell you," he replied with a half-smile.

"Christian told me you like lamb chops, so I hope you brought your appetite," I cracked a smile as I watched my husband hang their jackets in the closet.

"I'm ready to eat whatever you're serving," Kristofer said, licking his lips. I creased my brows, and Christian punched him in the arm. "What?" Kristofer blurted out, looking at Christian with his lips curled. "All I'm saying is dinner smells good," he laughed.

"Excuse us," Christian led Kristofer into his office and slammed the door. A few moments later, I heard scuffling. I peeped my head around the corner through the French glass door and noticed he was pinning Kristofer against the wall by the collar, "Don't disrespect my wife like that," he said, clenching his teeth.

Kristofer pushed Christian. "Disrespect, you're the last person that needs to be talking disrespect; get off me," he retorted, smoothing the wrinkles out of his shirt.

I stood in the hallway waiting to see what either would say. I stood motionless. The sounds of Christian's office phone interrupted their conversation, and he answered the phone out of breath. "Christian Powell," he said as he listened attentively, making verbal head nods before disconnecting. "This is not the time or the place. I just got the call we were waiting for, so let's have dinner and discuss this later. Can we agree to be civil and take care of our deal later?" he said, looking at Kristofer.

I managed to tiptoe back to the kitchen and threw on some oven mitts opening the oven to look busy as I seized the main entrée. Christian and his brother emerged into the kitchen and acted like everything was fine between them. Throughout dinner, I wondered what deal they had together, but I didn't want to ruin dinner. Despite Kristofer's unsettling comments, the evening turned positive, and we all enjoyed ourselves. Whatever dispute my husband and his brother were going through, I decided to put it out of my mind; for now, I was not going to get into the middle of two feuding siblings.

I'm glad dinner is over, I thought as I put away leftovers in the kitchen but was interrupted by the phone. The sound of the ringtone was a dead giveaway that it was Madison, and I was instantly annoyed. I rolled my eyes. *I don't have time for this right now*, I thought. I'd been avoiding her calls since I left her house the other day. After the second day of telling her that I was busy and would call back, I thought she'd get the hint and stop calling, but she was relentless. Finally, I took a deep breath and let out an exasperated sigh before answering, "Hey, Madison."

Before I could continue speaking, she cut me off. "I know you said you were going to call me back, but I can't keep waiting," she huffed. "We need to talk."

"About the other day, Madison, I'm sorry. I was angry and not myself," I rolled my eyes. I didn't have the chance to process my emotions, much less to think about hers. "I have a lot going on right now. Christian and I are dealing with our issues and sorting things out." I paused when I heard her weeping on the other end of the phone.

"I get it – it's alright. Neither of us anticipated having sex, but I love you, Essence," she cried.

I held the phone against my ear and stared into space wide-eyed; I was speechless and silent for a few minutes before speaking, "But I'm married, Madison. So, it was my fault for sleeping with you. I was very vulnerable and made a bad judgment call."

I assumed the blame because I didn't need any extra stress. "So, if I have to let go of our friendship because you're incapable of only being my friend, I will," I responded, pressing my lips together.

There was a slight hesitation in her speech. "You know what, you're right; I don't know what came over me," Madison said, changing the subject, "When are you planning on taking a pregnancy test?"

"I was planning on taking a test today." I paused for a moment before speaking. "I do need to go, though. I'll catch up with you later, yeah?"

"Alright, Essence," Madison hung up, and her tone was confirmation enough for me to know she wasn't accepting my request, but she would be alright eventually.

My stomach started feeling queasy again. Suddenly I felt faint. I sat down on the barstool at the kitchen island and picked up a piece of mail, using it as a fan. I was stalling long enough, and it was apparent that something was going on. Finally, I mustered up enough energy, put on some shoes, and headed out the door. I pulled into the parking lot of the local drugstore, and before I could park completely, I opened the door and threw up chunks of dinner. I moved my car to another parking space to prevent myself from stepping in the vomit and ran into the store and down the family planning aisle. I looked over a few pregnancy brands and picked up a test. I sat in silence as I drove back home, thinking of the outcome.

It's ironic how all I ever wanted was to start a family with Christian, but now that I was sitting on the toilet minutes away from getting results that could potentially change my life, I was scared shitless. I urinated on the stick, then sat the pregnancy test down on the sink. Eventually, I got up and paced back and forth. The sound of the door alarm beeping startled me, and I screamed out. "Hey babe," as I walked over to the stairs and looked at Christian, who was walking in the door.

"Yes, honey, you need something," he calmly asked. Then, I heard him locking the door shut and turning on the alarm for the evening.

"Babe, hurry up quick. I'm upstairs," I shouted back at him as I walked back into the bathroom and picked up the pregnancy test. Unfortunately, the writing was on the wall before the test results were in, but the double line on the pregnancy test confirmed it.

My heart was in my throat, and my palms were moist as I picked up the test and handed it to Christian as he walked into the bathroom with his lips curled up. I managed to crack a half smile and gave him the test. I felt my cheeks get flushed as the tears welled up in my eyes.

"What's this?" He asked as he took the pregnancy test from me, looking at the results. *Maybe this the blessing we needed to get our marriage back on track,* I thought, but my excitement quickly subsided as I noticed the color of his skin go from light caramel to a pale gray as he mumbled, "You're pregnant?" with furrowed brows. And just like that, in a matter of seconds, I was worried about how our next chapter of life would be raising a family.

"Have you been taking your birth control?" Christian covered his mouth with his hand, pacing the floor. Then, he covered his eyes, "It can't be, right? Did you try taking another test?"

"No, but I can take one to confirm," I responded as Christian sat down on the toilet, panting. "You don't seem happy. You were told you can't have kids, but here's proof you can; I would think you'd be happy."

He cracked a smile and pinched his nose. "No—I'm happy; I'm just shocked. I thought I couldn't have kids." We both stared at the pregnancy test again. "You need to take another pregnancy test so we can confirm it's right." He hopped up and headed to the door.

"Where are you going?" I creased my brows.

"To grab another test and non-alcoholic champagne; if the test says positive again, we can celebrate." He winked and left out the house.

I exhaled and looked back at the test and smiled. I walked into the nursery and sat in the rocking chair, looking around at what I manifested. I closed my eyes, imagining the sound of the baby whining. I rocked back and forth in the chair, waiting for Christian to return. After a short time, the doorbell rang. I tilted my head; *why didn't he use the key?* I thought and got up and headed to the front door. Opening the door, "You got the test?" I turned away, walking back up the stairs.

"Essence," Kristofer called out and stood at the door.

I turned around, recognizing it was Kristofer and not my husband, Christian.

I walked back to the door and peeped my head out, "Is something wrong? Christian should be back in a few."

"No, I wasn't here for Christian; I came to speak to you," he turned his head, squinting to see down the street. His behavior seemed suspicious.

I furrowed my brows, "Me, why?" I rested my hands on my waist.

"Can I come in for a second; it's important?" Kristofer glanced to the side.

He made me nervous, and I nodded, "No, Christian will be here soon," I ran my hands through my hair, "What's on your mind?" I leaned against the door, not to seem worried.

"It's Christian; he's been lying to you," his hands steepled, "Christian's not who he says he is; who she says she is," Kristofer corrected himself.

I shifted my eyes left and right, "What are you talking about?" I leaned forward.

"My brother he—he's transitioning to become a man. He has surgery tomorrow to start the process," he spoke rapidly.

After hearing the words transitioning to becoming a man, I failed to hear everything he was saying. I held my palms up, "Wait—wait," I placed my hand on my chest. My head started to spin. I swallowed hard, "No, no; that can't be true," I grabbed the door, closed it, and Kristofer placed his foot in the doorway and stopped it from closing completely.

"I know it sounds crazy, and I'm sure you don't believe me," he reached in this pocked and retrieved a medicine bottle, "Here's a prescription med; crush this up, and place it into a drink. Then, when he's asleep, go into his underwear and check."

"I'm not giving my husband any drugs; are you crazy?" I pushed the door to close it, and Kristofer threw the pills through the small opening before it shut.

I picked up the bottle, put it in my pocket, and sat down on the stairs. Narrowed-eyed, thinking about the story Kristofer just shared, this can't be for real; they argued earlier. Could he be trying to poison my husband? I clenched my jaw, recalling all the lies Christian told me, him disappearing without reason; what if this was true? I gagged.

The knobbed turned, and Christian walked in, "What's wrong, baby?" he grabbed my hand and helped me off the stairs. He handed me the bag from the drugstore, "Here's another test," he smiled and kissed my forehead.

I looked at the bag, unmoved; I grabbed it and headed to the bathroom. "Where's the champagne?" Small talk, Essence, Kristofer delivered the worst news of your life, and champagne is all you can think about, not the pregnancy or Christian's unfathomable truth. Shouldn't I be going off?

"Oh, I'm sorry it slipped my mind; I was too busy looking for the pregnancy test aisle," Christian walked into the bathroom and rested against the sink.

"Gotcha," I flashed a half-smile, "So, you're excited?" I scanned his face trying to detect his mood; he's become hard to read. Christian clutched his hands behind his head, blew his cheeks with air, and then released. I observed his emotions; he was aloof. I tried to distinguish if I saw any feminine traits, but it was hard to recognize any.

We continued to wait, and I thought, *what if Kristofer was lying; the story seemed too drastic.* Besides, how did Christian go this long without me detecting that he was transitioning? So, my unborn child had to be Christian's, right? *Who else could it be?* I thought, trembling.

"What's wrong, honey?" Christian held my hand, trying to calm me, "Everything is going to be alright," he pulled me closer to embrace me, "You're shaking?" He looked into my eyes.

I looked down at the pregnancy test; like before, both lines were positive; my body went limb.

"Whoa, have a seat, Essence. Are you sure you're alright?" Christian grabbed the disposable cup from the linen closet and filled it with water, "Here, drink this."

I took a few sips of water and smiled, "Thank you, I think I'm just tired," I emptied the cup and tossed it into the trash, "Let's go to bed."

We walked into the bedroom, and I got undressed. "Are you going to undress?" I looked at Christian.

"Eventually, I will; I want to make sure you're alright before I do," he sat down on the bed.

I once disregarded Christian's idiosyncrasies, undressing in the bathroom and locking the door as patterns of obsessive-compulsive disorder, but I now was questioning everything. I shook my head; I needed to know if Kristofer was telling the truth. "Wait, aren't we going to celebrate?" I perked up.

"I forgot the champagne, remember?" Christian stood up and sat beside me on the bed.

"I know, but we have wine; I'll go grab it," I grabbed the robe and slid my feet into the slippers.

Christian yelled out as I was halfway out of the room, "Babe, are you sure?" I heard the bathroom door close.

Typical, when I'm out of the room, now you want to undress, I thought, walking into the kitchen to grab the wine. I took the prescription bottle out of my robe pocket. Then, after reading the side effects, I crushed two pills and put it into Christian's glass. After that, I decided to take extreme measures, taking action without asking questions. I had been the naïve wife for too long. Although I did not want to believe Kristofer, my intuition knew something more was up, and since a baby was at stake, I desperately needed the truth.

I headed upstairs; Christian was undressed, staring at me, ginning, "Pregnant women shouldn't drink," he teased, reaching for the wine glass I held out.

"I think we can make an exception tonight," I smirked, "So, what do we cheers to?" I held my wine glass in the air.

"To love, marriage, and new life," we clinked wined glasses; Christian gulped his wine and leaned closer to rub my belly. Clenching my jaw, I stood still and sipped my wine as he continued to rub on me. "I hope it's a boy."

Spitting my wine out, I said, "A boy?" I curled my lip, then closed my eyes, remembering to remain poised. I did not want to act any differently. I smiled, "Why don't you want to be a girl-dad?" I smiled and drank the rest of my wine.

"No, boys are better," Christian laughed. Nevertheless, he was surprisingly confident, as though he knew girls weren't better.

I took the wine glasses, placed them on the nightstand, and I slid underneath the covers.

Restless, I lay in bed while Christian slept peacefully. I wrapped my arm around Christian, pulled him closer, and felt him flinch. I exhaled, turning over to look at the clock. How long will it take before he is asleep? The time gradually passed, and I caught myself dozing off a few times and shook myself awake.

Finally, I heard Christian snoring. He was a light sleeper, so I knew he was in a deep sleep since he hardly snored. He laid on his back; I leaned closer and waved my hand over his eyes, but nothing. I kissed his lips softly to see if my touch would awaken him, but he was immobile. I pressed my eyelids together; my next move would change everything. I inhaled, then slid my hand underneath the cover and into my husband's underwear. Kristofer was lying; the texture of his penis felt like his flesh and was flaccid. I smiled, but my conscious urged me to keep going since I was already in his underwear. This time, I squeezed tight enough to hurt him, but Christian did not move. To cast out more doubt, I patted his penis, and it moved out of position. Finally, I lifted what I thought to be his dick out of his underwear. I curled my lip in disgust as I examined the flaccid, 6-inch silicon shaft with skin folds and subtle asymmetrical testicles. It felt and looked natural, except it was my hand; therefore, it couldn't be real.

I panicked; I wanted to shriek, wake his ass up! But that would be way too easy. His lies impacted not only me but my unborn child; I needed a plan. There was so much to uncover. Christian was not the father of my child, and I needed to know the absolute truth. Kristofer eagerly wanted to come off as the truth-telling, knight and shining armor, but I know he was more involved in the elaborate scheme because I had to be fucking him. It is payback time!

Christian had made a fool of me one too many times, but this time, I'd play the fool a little longer to make an even bigger fool out of him!

Printed in the USA
CPSIA information can be obtained
at www.ICGtesting.com
LVHW101539090823
754669LV00023B/88